Vivienno Frank Jr.

OUTPOST ALTO VISTA

and other Cosmic Horrors from Aruba

OUTPOST ALTO VISTA
and other Cosmic Horrors from Aruba

First Printing: October, 2020

ISBN: 978-1-71650-270-5

Publisher: **Roman Six Publishing**
Tanki Flip 52 A
Noord,
Aruba
romansix@gmail.com

Edited by: **Jim Canaday**
themagicportal@gmail.com

Layout & Cover Design: **Vivienno L. Frank Jr.**

"The oldest and strongest emotion of mankind is fear,
and the oldest and strongest kind of fear
is fear of the unknown."

Howard Philip Lovecraft
American writer (1890 – 1937)

Prologue by the author

In 1972, at the age of 13, I read my first true horror story: Bram Stoker's Dracula. Two weeks of sleepless nights were the result. However, after conquering those two weeks of Post Traumatic Stress Disorder, I went back to the library for more. A small pocketbook caught my attention, not because of the title *Griezelverhalen* (Dutch for Horror Stories), but because of the author's name: H. P. Lovecraft.

That name somehow struck a chord. To me, at that time a young boy from Aruba, it had an ominous ring to it. A strange curiosity for the book's content took over in an unexplainable way. To this day, 47 years later, if my memory serves me right, I can still recall its front cover: an abstract painting of a dark castle. Sort of, I think.

I finished the book in one weekend. Back then, I didn't know there were several names for different types of horror genres, but I instantly felt this was totally unlike anything I had experienced. As a kid I saw most classic horror on TV, the likes of Dracula, Frankenstein, The Werewolf, The Mummy, and many more. Although always scary, I always knew in the back of my mind that it wasn't real; except for that Dracula fella of course, after reading the book. This however, was different. This was horror on a total different scale, dealing with fears of the strongest kind: the fear of the unknown; that what lurks in the vastness of space and time; of those able to transcend dimensions unknown to mankind, and for which there still isn't sufficient scientific proof of either their existence or inexistence, except for the testimonies of those that experienced the true mysterious 'bump in the night'. Many years later, I realized there existed a name for all this: *Cosmic Horror*. That fateful book I read so many years ago, *Griezelverhalen*, was written by its inventor, Howard Phillips Lovecraft.

So what defines *Cosmic Horror*. To me it's the insignificance of man, and especially, man's awareness of its own irrelevance with respect to the grand scheme of the cosmos. We float on a speck of dust in an infinite universe. Instinctively, we *know* there *must* exist *others* out there. The lack of knowledge of what we're dealing with, however, terrifies us immensely. Since ancient times, we suspect that we are probably just crawling at the bottom of the cosmic food chain; all those in upper echelons were considered *Gods*. In modern times, science gives us the arrogance to dismiss those *Ancient Ones* as mere myths and to pretend that we're the masters of our own fate; yet still, the knowledge that at any given moment a big rock from outer space can obliterate our existence, is as frightening as the ignorance of what really lurks there in deep space. Are we still here by sheer luck, or because *others* have been, or still are, being merciful with us? Or perhaps, and this may be even worse, because *they* still haven't found a way to make contact or to permeate into our dimensions and regions? Who is to know? As Lovecraft himself so eloquently stated: "We live on a placid island of ignorance in the midst of black seas of infinity, and it was not meant that we should voyage far."

Since my mid-twenties, I have dabbled with ideas, and jotted down concepts and story lines. Thanks to my brother, who always kept pushing me and telling me I should seriously consider to start publishing all those creepy bits and pieces, I began in my early forties to compile all those weird ideas into stories and novels. Besides writing in my native Papiamento and Dutch, English to me has always been the de facto language for narrating creepy stuff. Unfortunately, English always remained a second language to me, and I have to give a big word of gratitude to my good friend Jim Canaday in the US, for going through this collection of short stories with a magnifying glass, filtering out a lot of 'impurities' in the course of time. Obviously, like the Argentineans say, *siempre le faltará un pelo para completar al gato* (there will always be missing a hair to complete the cat). Nevertheless, I hope the end result is to your satisfaction.

This is my first collection of cosmic horror written in English. In here, you will find five stories that provoked the classic "where the hell do you get all this from, do you sleep at night?" reaction from my brother. I thank him for that, and I hope that you will enjoy these five stories as much as I have enjoyed writing them.

Vivienno 'Vi' Frank Jr.
Aruba, October 2020

Cosmic Horrors Found In This Book:

Dedicated to those who dare to dance, even when labeled insane by those unable to hear the music.

Outpost Alto Vista

Since the dawn of time, certain places on earth have been experienced by people as strange, mysterious, and even somewhat ominous and possessing a weird aura. The reason has always eluded me, as I'm sure it has eluded almost everyone involved in these matters since even the first time such a place has been pointed out millennia ago. Even if a civilization passed away, the remnants of their worshipping still remind the new occupants that the place had a special meaning. The reason sometimes remained unexplained to the new conquerors, but they kept observing these locations with a certain awe and respect.

The ancient inhabitants of Britain had their Stonehenge. The elder tribes in the Peruvian highlands had their Nazca plains with their mysterious lines. The Mayas their Tikal, the bushmen of the Kalahari their sacred tree, and the aborigines in central Australia their Ayers Rock. So it came as no surprise that even the tiny island of Aruba in the Southern Caribbean, had its own mystifying location on top of an elevation at the north coast named "Alto Vista". Spanish for "elevated view", I later discovered.

I first encountered Alto Vista during one of my numerous cross bike country tours. The road to it was lit with religious crosses and symbols on the side representing the different stages of the journey of Christ to his crucifixion. It intrigued me immensely, and upon arriving at the top, the view all the way to the rugged North coast in the distance instantly mesmerized me with the huge waves splashing against its rocky formations. A plain littered with giant boulders. As if a giant had left his marbles scattered around after playing and left to unknown destinations. I had read about this site in tourist manuals before arriving in Aruba to fulfill my 5 year tour of duty as a psychologist under contract with the government, but nothing had prepared me for the sudden impact this particular view may have on the psyche. I immediately felt a deep moment of awe, a spiritual moment of tranquility even with the strong wind battering my face. Right there and then I understood instantly why the early settlers of Aruba had chosen this site to build the first Chapel on Aruba in the mid-eighteenth century. At least, that's what I thought until one day I met Jose Gonzalez, a journalist whose enigmatic and traumatic experience shocked the foundations of my most inner beliefs with uncompromising brutality.

It is not my habit to write down experiences or sessions with patients. Somehow in this particular case I was unable to suppress an unexplainable urge. Therefore, I write this down as accurately as possible so a record may remain of past events, an indicator of what the future may bring, and a testimony that at that time I was a sane individual. I wrote the following accounts in the hope that whatever happens in the future does not pass unnoticed for at least one member of mankind, may God rest his brave soul.

Session 1

My name is Dr. Simon Gupta, neurosurgeon and clinical psychologist, and the day I met Jose Gonzalez was a day like any other. It started with the usual hassle of bringing my wife to work and the children to school. For such a small island, Arubian traffic can inflict the same frustration as any major big city traffic in the morning. I was late and rushed hastily into my office, ignoring my secretary and some old lady sitting in the waiting room. There he was. Sitting in the patient's chair. Staring into an unknown void. Jose Ramon Ignacio Gonzalez.

The night before our first meeting I studied his file extensively. Born from a Venezuelan father and Aruban mother on April 24, 1964. Highly intelligent it seemed, as he graduated from Aruba's top high school at the early age of sixteen as number 4 of the all time best students. His strong mathematical skills inclined him to start studying astrophysics at the Royal University of Utrecht in the Netherlands. Much to his parents dismay, he dropped out of school 6 months before finishing his final thesis. He suddenly disappeared in the fall of 1986. During that mysterious period in his life up to 1990, he never contacted any member of his family and friends. As sudden as he had vanished, he appeared back on the social radar screen in the spring of '91 and enrolled at the same university in Utrecht with journalism as major. He aced it in three years flat, and started a very successful career as a journalist for some of Europe's major magazines. In mid 2005 he came back to his native island to attend his father's funeral and never went back. Soon thereafter he made his name with the local media, became a highly admired journalist, radio commentator and TV host, and enjoyed relative fame and fortune until those dramatic events that started about 6 months ago and ultimately landed him in my office.

My apologies to him for being late went barely noticed by him, as he just hummed something that seemed an acknowledgement when I sat in front of him. My extended hand as a greeting gesture went equally unanswered. I decided not to be disturbed by his silent antagonism, and made myself comfortable in my chair. The clock on the wall was ticking. Its sound gradually swelled to become the only distinguishable background noise. At a certain point I pretended to be somewhat uninterested in him, and faked slowly dozing off. Nevertheless he managed to make me jump by unexpectedly breaking silence :

```
[The following is a literal transcript of
our first session]
JG : "Is it ok if I call you Simon?"
Me : "That's all right if you prefer"
JG : "Goop-ta leaves little choice, don't
you think?"
Me : "Maybe... it's Gupta by the way..."


[Minutes of intense silence followed]


JG : "Do you believe in God Simon?"
Me : "Well yes I do. Why? Don't you?"
JG : "Does it matter if I do?"
Me : "Of course it does"
JG : "Hmmm... Interesting concept"
Me : "Why is that?"
JG : "Hmmm..."
```

Here he shifted his position on his chair to face me straight on. His eyes locked into mine, and again an unbearable moment of silence followed. I became uneasy. My left hand slowly reached for a secret button under my chair's left arm.

[Transcript continues]

JG : "I was wondering upon a philosophical question for quite some time. Maybe you can help me out by giving your highly academic opinion."

Me : "Well you certainly have me intrigued Mr. Gonzalez. Can I call you Jo? It is Jo isn't it?"

JG : "It depends. My friends call me Jo. Are you my friend Simon?"

Me : "I certainly hope so. Well? Can I call you Jo?"

[Long period of silence]

JG : "No."

Me : "Uh... ok. What do you prefer to be called then, Mr. Gonzalez, Mr. Jose Gonzalez, or Señor Jose Ramon Ignacio Gonzalez?"

[Silence again, sudden sound of chair moving]

Me : "Excuse me, but where do you think you're going? Hey! Amigo! What the he—"

JG : "I think this has been enough for our first meeting."

Me : "But your time hasn't finished yet."

JG : "Oh, but yours certainly has. Goodbye Simon."

[Footsteps. Knocking sound on the door. Secretary opens the door.]

Secr. : "Finished so soon Mr. Gonzalez?"

JG : "I'm afraid yes dear. Is my aunt still here?"

Secr. : "Well yes. She has been waiting here all along."

Aunt : "Everything all right Josito?"

JG : "Yes auntie. Will you take me home now please?"

Aunt : "Yes dear. Let's go. Goodbye Doctor, goodbye Ms. Henriquez."

Secr. : "Goodbye Ms. Gonzalez. Please do remember our next session is next week, same day, same time."

Aunt : "Thank you dear, I sure will."

And there I was. Somewhat flabbergasted. That first meeting certainly did not go as I had expected. I remember wondering at that moment what kind of a man this fellow was. The comments in his file, made by his general practitioner before he was referred to me, indicated loss of memory, depression, maybe psychosis, due to some mysterious traumatic experience that happened to him on the night of June 21st, 2009. The early signs of psychological disturbances were all there. Lack of sleep at night, restlessness, easily irritable, long periods of absentness of mind. He repeatedly claimed that something of unspeakable horror happened to him. It's there, he claims, if he could only remember it.

I closed his file on my lap, and just sat there for another half hour. Puzzling. Thinking on how to approach this man, and, last but not least, how to avoid another embarrassing moment like this first session. My ego had been dented, and a bruised ego is a terrible guide to make decisions.

❦ ❦ ❦ ❦

Session 2

A week had passed. One with many nights wondering about the strange feeling this case had brought. The spine tingling sensation that you were about to step into quicksand. Jose was my second patient that day, and I regretted that the moment my first patient left my office. In retrospective I admit I have caused more harm to my patients than good by scheduling any of them on the same day as Jose. I should have stuck to attending him alone on those days.

```
[Transcript of session number 2, November
11th, 2009]


Me : "Good morning, how are we feeling
today."
JG : "Depends, Simon, depends. It all
depends on how you're feeling today."
Me : "I'm feeling great! Super charged as
they say, ready to take on the world, and
I see that you are feeling quite energized
yourself."
```

JG : "Remember how our last meeting ended Simon?"

Me : "Yes, how so"?

JG : "Your time ended rather abruptly don't you think?"

Me : "Well, if you want to call it so, yes, but ..."

JG : "Ever wondered during the last couple of days why that came to be?"

[Silence]

JG : "I don't think an encore is on your agenda today, is it?"

Me : [sigh] "Not really, no, tell me what you have in mind for today..."

JG : "You still haven't answered me, do you know why things went wrong last time?"

Me : "I have an idea."

JG : "Which is?"

Me : "I suppose I offended you somehow, but ..."

JG : "You suppose?"

Me : "I'm sure I did, I'm just not sure when and how."

JG : "Hmmmm ... Interesting."

[Silence, scuffling sound of chair moving]

Me : "Ok, no need to walk away again sir, I think it's when I mocked you with how you would wish to be addressed. I think I offended your intelligence somehow. Honest to God, that's what I think, if not so, then I'm lost here."

JG : "Hmmm … interesting, very interesting."

[Sound of chair moving]

JG : "Well, now that we have settled that, let's move on to where we were before you became rude, shall we?"

Me : "Most certainly, ... euh ..."

JG : "You can call me Jose... Jo will also do fine."

Me : "Ok Jose, let's move on please, you were trying to discuss something with me last time, if I'm not mistaken."

JG : "Ooh yes, my philosophical question."

Me : "Yep! That was it. Proceed please."

[Silence]

JG : "What would you say is best. Living relatively happy not knowing you were living a lie, or living miserably but in absolute certainty you know the truth."

[Long silence. Faint sound of clock ticking in the background]

JG : "Well?"

Me : "I'm not sure ... it's uh... an unusual question. Can you elaborate with a more precise example?"

JG : "You believe in God you said."

Me : "I certainly do."

JG : "Are you happy with how things are being managed by him at the moment?"

Me : "There is room for improvement, I admit, but in a certain way, I'm happy, yes, he has his reasons why he manages things as they are at the moment."

JG : "And yet ... you're a man of science ... aren't you?"

Me : "Yes I am. Most definitely I may add."

JG : "Hmmm ... interesting."

[Silence. Throat being cleared]

JG : "Suppose for a moment you get the opportunity to trade that relative happiness for the absolute truth. The absolute knowledge of what's really out there. But it comes at a price. The price being the forfeiting of all hope as described by all major religions, would you do it?"

Me : "I must admit I've never even pondered on that possibility as it seems to me impossible to attain, but supposing for a moment that such a chance did occur. Hmmm, interesting. I may be tempted as a man of science."

JG : "Even if you knew you were running the risk of losing your sanity? Of living for the rest of your life in paranoid despair or unhappiness? Would you still?"

Me : [long sigh] "I must again admit that my curiosity as a scientist may on the long run take the upper hand. But why are you asking me this Jo, is there something you wish to tell me?"

[Short silence followed by sound of chair being moved]

JG : "Yes."

[Silence followed by sound of chairs moving]

Me : "Why don't you tell me then Jo. Let's talk about this as grown men."
JG : "I can't..."

[Silence. Clock ticking in background again noticeable]

Me : "Why not?"
JG : "I can't. I can't remember it. I have this deep conviction you see, that I've stumbled upon something. Something mindboggling and of unspeakable horror... all my senses tell me that, and I'm certain that if I manage one day to remember what it was, that I will lose my sanity, as I'm convinced that I know a terrible and absolute truth. It's like I'm trying to open a door by pulling while the sign clearly says push. And yet, I'm unable to push. Something terrible happened that night. Something terrible that no human mind should ever behold. If I could only... aargghh!"

[Gargling throat noises; sudden loud movement of chair]

JG : "I'm afraid our time is up again Simon. Goodbye, I'll keep in touch, please don't call, I'll call you."

[Footsteps. Door opening and closing]

I remember he took my hand and shook it when he left. Progress has been made in that respect. There I was again. Left behind, sitting with his open file as an incomplete clue in my lap. I decided to once again pass through the police report about that night. According to officer first class Dennis Maduro, various 911 calls had entered almost simultaneously from residents on the leeward side of the water tank hill at Alto Vista. The residents in the neighborhood that called the police reported hearing terrible inhuman screams coming from the direction of the uphill Alto Vista chapel further North. After being dispatched, Officer Maduro was one of the first ones who arrived at the scene.

It was 3:30 AM. Maduro reports that besides the usual howling winds, all else seemed quiet. He checked around the chapel, when a sudden bone penetrating sub-human scream of unparalleled intensity was heard, not only by him, but also by aspirant officer Tromp who had just arrived on the scene. They found Jose tangled in the nearby *hubada*[1] bushes. His clothes and skin were lacerated by the inch long *hubada* thorns on numerous places. Maduro described Jose Gonzalez as screaming in total hysteria, completely incoherent, shivering all over his body; with eyes wide open staring constantly in the distance and not even noticing the two officers desperately trying to communicate. The two officers decided to take him to the hospital, where he was left in custody of the ER at 4:05 AM. Their initial conclusions: probably advert reaction to drugs conducive to paranoid delusional behavior.

His medical report however, made up by Dr. Petrocchi, showed indications of a more disturbing nature. Shortly after he was left, Jose Gonzalez started to bleed profusely through his

---

[1] Acacia Tortuosa. A native tree with very large thorns.

mouth, ears, and anus. He was rushed immediately to the operating chambers of Dr. Horacio Oduber Hospital where a visually shocked Dr. Petrocchi barely saved his life at 5:10 AM. His conclusions were inconclusive. Although there were definitely signs of drug abuse, the hemorrhagic bleedings were not caused by interactions with these. There were also no signs of sexual abuse whatsoever. Nevertheless, something or someone, had definitely ruptured Jose's insides in a most unusual way.

❧ ❧ ❧ ❧

Session 3

Jo never complied thereafter with any made appointment for almost 3 weeks. No matter what the reason, his aunt dutifully called every time to cancel or reschedule an appointment, stating that Jo was very sick and that she feared the worst. No matter how we tried to contact him over the phone, Jo never came himself to respond, and left everything in the old lady's hand. We once tried a surprise visit, but it was in vain. Jo's aunt stood guard at the door, answered all our enquiries about Jo's wellbeing, but never gave in an inch. Jo didn't want to speak to us, she said, and she was not to break her vow to respect his private life. If Jo wanted help, Jo must show this himself, she stated wisely, otherwise everything would have been in vain.

So, understandably, we were all shocked when early one Monday morning we found Jo sitting outside the clinic building. He approached me rather quietly and with a solemn stare he just uttered the words "it's time Simon. I'm ready when you are". While I took Jo straight into my office I told my secretary to start

calling patients and to reschedule them for at least an hour past
their scheduled appointment. He sat down and stared at me in his
accustomed disturbing fashion.

```
[Transcript of session 3, December 7th,
2009]


Me: "This is most unexpected and yet most
welcome Jo. You have my undivided
attention."


[Silence]


Me: "Would you like some water, coffee,
anything else before we start Jo?"


[Silence]


Me: "Very well Jo, take your time, I'm ready
when you are."


[Silence. Sound of clock ticking. Some
outside noises filtering through]


JG: "I wonder why you never stood up for
yourself after graduating high school."
Me: "I beg your pardon?"
JG: "You never wanted to become a
psychologist in the first place. You came
to like it in due course of time, yes, but
the truth is you always wanted to become a
fireman. So why didn't you stood up for
yourself back then when they forced you to
follow an academic career?"
```

[Throat clearing]

Me: "Nobody forced me to do anything Jo. Is this what you want to see me for?"

JG: "Your mother did. In fact she made quite an issue about it with the rest of your family who joined into her crusade to bring you to the right path, to make you see the light so to speak."

[Silence]

Me: "I... euh..."

JG: "Never mind torturing your mind to find the right words to steer this session back to where you thought it would go when you brought me in here this morning. Don't you find it interesting how I came to know these things?"

[Some nervous laughter]

Me: "You know nothing Jo, it's all in your head. I never wanted to be a fireman. Now can we proceed with what's important here, your wellbeing?"

JG: "Okay, let's take this up a notch. Do you recall when you were chased by a pack of wild dogs when you were 11? You ran your heart out in the bush, and finally you had to jump into a big cactus swatch. You were in agonizing pain from all the needles sticking everywhere into your whole body, but at least the dogs were kept at bay. Finally, after what seemed an eternity to you, the fire brigade searching for you found and rescued you. It was there and then that you became fascinated with becoming a fireman."

[Silence; some chair movement]

JG: "Well? Intrigued Simon or shall I change gear again?"

Me: "How... how... who... who gave you this information?"

JG: "Aha! I see... the science man takes over again. There has to be a logical explanation isn't it? The how replaced by the who. I can tell you more if you like. I can tell you things that happened during your years as a student in New England that nobody back in your hometown knows. But then again you would suggest that I have spoken to many more people than just your folks back home. So why not take this up another notch, why not talk about something that only you can possibly know."

[Clock ticking; silence; humming sound of tape recorder mechanism overpowering]

Me: "Ok, as you wish. I must admit you play the part of mentalist very well; had me fooled for a while, but it can all be explained. You see, I almost forgot that you are indeed a top notch investigative journalist. In the time between our last session and this one, a pro like you may have done some interesting digging around indeed. Impressive, Jo, come to think of it, most impressive."

JG: "Mm-hm, go on, you're about to propose a bet."

Me: "How the hell? Ha! Damn! You're indeed gifted with a very keen sense of perception. Well yes I was indeed going to propose something. Well if you're that good Jo, tell me, what was I going to propose?"

JG: "You were going to propose a bet, which is to give me one, and only one, more chance to take me serious. The bet is I am to tell something only you could know. Something, that absolutely only you could know, as you are certain you have never told anyone before. If I'm unable to do that right now, in this instance, I lose the bet and I am to agree never to insinuate that I am able to perceive things in an unexplainable manner. Am I right Simon?"

[Silence]

Me: "Oh come on Jo, that wasn't that hard to read on my face, was it? Well yes [voice getting angry] let's have it then, let's play your stupid game, let's pretend you're indeed a true mentalist, WHAT COULD YOU POSSIBLY TELL ME JO THAT ONLY I COULD KNOW!"

[Silence; sound of recorder slowly swelling]

Me: "Helllooooo Jo! [giggling voice] are you planning to stare me to death? I must admit that you have some impressive stare Jo. I guess even Houdini would be jealous, but you're going to need a little more than that to pry into my most inner secrets."

[Silence; sudden loud chair movement]

Me: "Oh God, what an act, stop it! I'm going to call it ..."

JG: "It's the day you lost your faith Simon... your faith in God."

[Voice sounds trance like]

[Sound of chair movement; sound of person sitting in chair]

JG: "It was a hot day in July. Summer vacation. A week or two after your 14th birthday. Your father gave you a BB rifle on your birthday. Your mother strongly disapproved, but your father made you promise never to use it on a living thing, never to kill anything, but to use it in true sportsmanship. You were fascinated at first honing your shooting skills, perfecting your aim, but after two weeks you got bored shooting at cans and plastic bottles. So one day, while you were wandering alone in the woods, you saw a dove sitting on a distant branch. It was quite far, maybe at the edge of the rifle's accuracy range, and you got tempted ... you wondered if it was possible to hit it. You took aim and you even thought it was impossible, totally impossible, that you would ever hit it anyway; so you squeezed the trigger... expecting not to harm the bird but just to scare it away, and to your horror you saw it drop to the ground. You ran and ran, it seemed ages before you reached the tree, and there it was, in the shadows by the roots, still alive and panting heavily, struggling and clinging to life, blood gushing from its beak... you cried in panic... you cried incessantly... until you dropped to your knees and started praying... praying like you never done before! You asked God to save the bird, you promised to do everything he wants for the rest of your life as long as he saved the bird, and through your tears you saw how the bird's breathing slowed down while his eye stared at you as if asking why. You were still holding it in your hands, the flood of tears washing the blood away. Finally it died... its eye questioning you no more."

[Silence; clock ticking; car horn in the distance]

JG: "You remained like that for quite some time, on your knees, the dead bird in your hands. And then you screamed, you asked God why! Why he allowed you to do this, why he didn't stop you, why he allowed the bullet to hit a one in a million shot, why he hadn't saved the bird, why you should have this burden on your soul, why, why, why! You sat there a long time before finally getting some sense of reality and getting a grip on yourself. At the end you buried the bird and went home. You never told anyone what had happened that day, but the images of the dying bird and the way it looked you in the eye haunted you for many nights, weeks, even months. It was, after all, the first time you have taken a life. It was not to be your last though."

[Long silence ... chair moving. Sound of footsteps fading and returning, sound pattern repeats itself for some time. Chair moves, sound of person sitting. Heavy sigh, very, very heavy sigh]

Me: "Jo..." [choking whispering voice] "...This... this...".

JG: "Is unbelievable, right? I know, I realize that."

[Silence for a long time; sound of tape recorder inner works]

Me: "Jo... Words elude me. During my whole career I have never ever encountered something like this. Please don't get me wrong, but I have to hear it from you. Since when are you aware of these extraordinary abilities?"

JG: "Since I recovered from that dreadful night. About a day or two after I was released from the Hospital. It started slowly. Like random voices in my head... for example I would happen to look at someone passing by and suddenly get images, voices, impressions. I slowly started experimenting and soon realized that if I paid attention I could fine tune these thoughts. It's sometimes like tuning to a distant radio station."

[Sudden chair movement, footsteps, door opens in distance and voices are heard]

[Distant voice] Me: "Martha could you please come in for a second?"

[Footsteps coming closer]

Me: "Martha please, I would like to try an interesting experiment here with Mr. Gonzalez, could you please take this piece of paper and write a ten digit number on it without letting Mr. Gonzalez see or peek what you write?"

Secr.: "Uh... ok, just any number?"

Me: "Yes, please, any random number that occurs to you."

[silence]

Secr.: "Ok, here you are."

Me: "No, don't give it to me, just keep the paper in front of you in such manner that neither of us can see it, and please keep looking at the numbers while you repeat them in your head."

Secr.: "Ok."

Me: "Jo are you ready?"

JG: "Yes... the numbers are 1018703927. The first 6 are her birth date in month, day, year. The last four is a combination of her age, 39, and address number, 27, respectively".

Secr.: "Oh my God! How... how..."

Me: "Thank you Martha, please."

Secr.: "But..."

Me: "Please Martha, that will be all for now, I'll explain later... please..."

[Footsteps; door closing; chair being moved]

JG: "Seen enough Simon?"

Me: "Yes."

JG: "This is no ordinary case isn't it? Will you help me?"

Me: "Do you want my help? Do you even need my help? Do you want help anyway?"

JG: "The voices are coming more often and they are getting stronger Simon. Lately, sometimes, I do not always manage to shut them down. Yes, I want your help. For some unexplainable reason I have felt the urge to request your services. Dr. Petrocchi, the physician who treated me at the hospital, insisted I seek further professional help, and suggested various names. The moment I heard yours I instantly knew it should be you. Up to now I have no explanation why..."

[Silence]

Me: "I will Jo, I will try to help. But you must promise me Jo that you will abide to my instructions".

JG: "Am I to blindly follow a blind man?"

Me: "I know what you mean Jo. I do not have any clue what has happened or is happening to you, but there must be a reason why your extraordinary insights told you to choose me, and I promise you I'll give it my best shot to get to the bottom of this."

JG: "I know Simon, I know... our time has finished for now, hasn't it?"

Me: "For now yes. Go home and rest as much as possible while I think things through. I will call you tomorrow and set a date for our next and most important session. By that time, I will have an initial strategy."

[Footsteps. Door opening and closing]

There I was. All alone. Flabbergasted, rocked to my bones, all previous beliefs shaken to their inner core. The office felt like a huge empty dome. My head felt like it was on the brim of exploding. What was I to make of what I had just witnessed?

This was just extraordinary! Absurd one may add, but the fact was that the statistical odds of such event happening at random was just short of nonexistent. I could go on and on rambling theories, but if anything made sense, the more I replayed everything in my head, the more I was convinced of the fact that somehow, something, an unknown phenomenon, has unlocked a hidden ability in Jo's mind, or had suddenly supplied him with that extraordinary ability.

Theories abound in the world of cognitive psychology discussing the seemingly vast untapped potential of the subconscious mind. Numerous experiments have been tried to prove that some of us indeed possess hidden "psychic" abilities of some sort, but all of these experiments have come up just short of what's statistically acceptable! A narrow margin of proof! But this... this has obliterated any uncertainty factor!

And there it was. As clear as a crystal ball. My "eureka" moment. Indeed I had no clue what has happened to Jo, or for the same value, what was happening to him, but the only option available that seemed obvious to me is to dig into that subconscious mind by means of regression hypnosis. It has been a while since I have practiced it, but I must give it a shot. Its practical value has been proven time after time in most cases.

I decided to call Jo that same evening. I explained to him exactly what I intended to do as a first step to get a foothold on what has proven to be a total mystery to both of us. Jo hesitated at first, but soon realized that certain risks had to be taken, and so agreed to be in my office by Friday afternoon at 2 o'clock. It seemed indeed like we were to take a random jump into a dark abyss, but other options weren't really around. Jo has to face what horrible events took place on that terrible night at Alto Vista.

❋ ❋ ❋ ❋

Epilogue

My name is Anna Gupta. I'm 18 years old, daughter of Dr. Simon Gupta, and what I am about to write may be the hardest and saddest thing I ever do in my life. I do this out of respect to my father, and also in order to solve a most ominous mystery. One day someone may read this whole manuscript and figure out what has transpired on that terrible Friday evening, which has filled me, and the rest of my family, with the greatest sorrow imaginable.

Up to this moment, as I'm penning these sentences, we have no knowledge whatsoever of the whereabouts of my father. It has been six months ago that, to use an old saying, it seemed the earth had mysteriously swallowed him. Vanished. As in thin air. He called home that Friday afternoon and the last person he spoke to was my mother, whom he told that he may come home very late, maybe even stay at the office for the weekend, as he was seeing a very interesting patient upon whom he was to conduct some extremely important experiments.

My mom, being the patient housewife she has always been, told us that all planned activities for the weekend we had with my father were off. To be continued in the next "coming soon event" as she jokingly put the news down. We were disappointed at first, but quickly refocused our attention to other activities, as we were used to dad sometimes having to deal with unexpected situations at work. What we never expected was how doom was to descend upon our house the following Monday morning.

Although it has been six months ago, I can still remember that moment I noticed that something terrible was happening as if it just had occurred yesterday. I was reading a book, and my peaceful surroundings were suddenly shredded by the most gut wrenching outcry of agony I've ever heard. I jumped up and raced downstairs, where I found my mother in total hysteria while Mrs. Henriquez, my father's loyal secretary, was trying to calm her down. Next to them there were two police officers. They bore disturbed looks on their faces. Something sinister has happened at my father's office, one of the officers told me. As he spoke a terrible buzzing sound built up in my ears, and I was told later that for a brief moment I had a total blackout.

The frantic ride to my father's practice was like a haze. Buildings, cars, pedestrians, all raced by wrapped in the all overpowering sound of the police car's siren. I had an arm around Maritza, my 16 year old sister, and we were both silent. The suddenness of it all, the inability to understand what was going on, the incapability to imagine what may have happened or what to expect, smothered any attempt at speech. We had lost all notion of time and space on a ride that seemed to have no end in sight.

Upon arrival the first thing that struck me was the huge amount of police and medical personnel around the building. Ambulances and police cars were everywhere. My sister and I were to remain in the car, but we quickly disobeyed that order. Before anyone noticed, we managed to escape and ran to enter the building, straight to my father's practice. What we encountered there goes beyond any human description possible.

Even now, after six months, I just have to close my eyes and I can see and smell it all again. Walls covered with blood, guts, and a strange greenish ooze that smelled as if a thousand rotten intestines had burst open at the same time. Pieces of clothing, books, furniture, all shredded and ripped; lying everywhere below a thin layer of a strange damp mist, equally greenish in color, emanating an even darker smell. The horrific details are endless, and I could go on and on describing them, but that would elude the main purpose why I'm putting all this on paper, which is to present you with the only evidence available of the tragic events that took place on that dreadful afternoon : the complete transcript of the tape bearing witness of the last session held between my father and his intriguing patient, Mr. Gonzalez.

❋ ❋ ❋ ❋

The Last Session

The following is the complete official transcript of the last session between my father and Mr. Jo Gonzalez, as retrieved by me from my father's internet backup system.

```
[Clicking sound of recorder starting.
Humming sound of inner mechanism.]

Dr. G: "How do you feel Jo."
JG: "Nervous but at ease."
Dr. G: "Now Jo, we have gone over the
procedures of this session a few times, but
```

it is important that, for the record, you state in your own words what is about to take place."

JG: "Hmm-hmm... well I'm about to be hypnotized by you, and while under hypnosis you will ask me questions that will relate to what happened that night. It is your intention to slowly take me to the time and place of the incident and try to make me remember as much as possible what happened. I understand that there is some inherent risk in this procedure, as the sudden memory of possible traumatic events may be too much to bear, but I'm willing to take that chance. Does that sum it up?"

Dr. G: "Pretty much. Couldn't have done it better. Now, you're also aware that I will administer you a drug that will put you in a very relaxed state, loosen up natural inhibitions, and allow you to open your mind to be more receptive to the hypnosis process."

JG: "Correct. You have also told me that in a very few occasions there may be adverse reactions, however that is a risk I'm willing to take. Go ahead doc... 'sin miedo'"

Dr. G: "Very well, let's proceed."

[Some scuffling sounds, period of silence]

Dr. G: "Ok. Now Jo, I'll now start a metronome and I want you to close your eyes, keep them closed unless I tell you not to, and for a while focus your attention on the sound and rhythm of it. Ok?"

JG: "Hmm-hmm."

Dr. G: "Very well, here we go."

[Ticking sound starts. About two minutes pass with only ticking sound on tape]

Dr. G: "Jo, from now on I would like you to focus on my voice, and my voice only. My voice will be the most important thing in this room. My voice will be the only thing important in your life. You will obey my voice at all times, as if there is nothing else that matters in this room... outside this room... In your life... on this planet... besides the single tone of what my voice has to say... you shall not speak nor move until my voice tells you to... you shall relax all muscles in your body while listening to my voice. You shall feel only the rhythm of my voice, which ticks along with the rhythm of your heart and your breathing. All slowing down. All slowing down... all slowing down. To that single sound of tick.. tock. Tick. Tock... tick... tock... tick... tock."

[Silence; sound of metronome in background]

Dr. G: "At the count of five Jo you will be completely and deeply asleep... surrounded by complete darkness... you are floating in a dark empty space in one... two... three... four... Five!"

[Silence; sound of metronome in background]

DR. G: "Where are you Jo?"

[Silence; sound of metronome in background]

Dr. G: "You may answer me Jo. Where are you?"

JG: "I... Don't know... it's dark. Very dark."

Dr. G: "That's right... you're floating in a completely dark place... there is no up. There is no down. There is no left... there is only right. There is only right. Turn to your right Jo."

JG: "Hmmm."

Dr. G: "Do you see the strip of light far away Jo?"

JG: "Hmm-hmm."

Dr. G: "I want you to slowly float to that light Jo. Slowly. The light is getting nearer... it's getting closer and closer... it's the light beneath a door Jo... do you see the door Jo?"

JG: "Yes."

Dr. G: "I want you to reach out and open that door Jo, and after you have opened it, I want you to step through it... it is still dark, but not that dark anymore, Jo. You see hills, and trees bathed softly in the faint light of the moon Jo. You hear the sea in the distance, you can smell the salt in the air. Close the door behind you Jo. You are now standing on the hilltop overlooking Alto Vista".

[Silence; sound of metronome in background]

Dr. G: "Where are you Jo"?

JG: "Alto Vista".

Dr. G: "Yes Jo. It's the night you went there for some reason on June 21st. Why were you there Jo?"

JG: "I don't know. I was driving around...
Late... I couldn't sleep, so I went for a
drive. I drove around the hotels, and
finally I drove up to the water tank on the
hill at Alto Vista."

Dr. G: "Why couldn't you sleep Jo?"

JG: "Lots of things on my mind..."

Dr. G: "Why stop at the water tank at Alto
Vista Jo?"

JG: "Wanted some peace and tranquility. To
enjoy the view of the Hotel and City lights.
Besides, needed to think things through
about a new report I was investigating about
Alto Vista."

Dr. G: "What about Alto Vista Jo..."

JG: "Strange things happening there
lately... rumors about mysterious sounds
and lights deep in the night... people
afraid to talk... afraid to go at dawn to
the chapel to pray as usual... as I couldn't
sleep I thought I might as well stay up and
observe that place."

Dr. G: "And? Did you observe anything?"

JG: "The wind was blowing, but at times, when
it calmed down, it carried strange distant
sounds to me ... often it resembled a distant
swarm of 'yeye' ... cicadas you know, those
you find in August. I knew this would have
been impossible at that time of year...
still though that was the sound... also,
when the cicadas subsided for a moment, I
could clearly hear some sort of chanting
coming from the direction of the chapel
behind the hills. I could see a strange faint
glow... an eerie light... soft greenish
glow... sometimes changing to pink, then
blue, then light green again..."

[Silence; sound of metronome in background]

Dr. G: "Go on Jose... what did you do then."

JG: "I... I... its intensity... the screech condensing to madness... a thousand 'yeyes' in my head... I... I had to lay on the ground... chants were blending into screams from afar... outcries for help... I... I crawled to a boulder while still trying to cover my ears... I felt my stomach... a sudden cramp... I tried to stand up and look over the boulder... a soft yet firm tremble on the ground permeated everything... the screeching rose to a sharp crescendo overpowering all senses... it all stopped suddenly, the screech, the screams, the chants, the tremble, a faint humming the only sound left... it was then that I... I... I managed to look over the boulder..."

[Silence; sudden noise of chairs and table moving, a loud bang, thumping sounds probably on the floor, wild frantic screaming]

Dr. G: "JO! JO! JOSE!... JOOO!... shit... SHIT!... Damn!"

[Scuffling sounds; screams; a slap; chairs falling; desk moving; faint screech in the distance...]

JG: "THE DOGS ARE COMING! THE DOGS ARE COMING! IT'S A PACK! THEY MUST HAVE HEARD MY SCREAM!"

Dr. G: "Get a grip on yourself JOSE... I COMMAND YOU! Listen to my..."

[Scuffling sounds; screams; a few slaps; chairs falling; desk moving; faint screech in the distance..]

Dr. G: "Jesus Christ! Jo! JO! ...let go of that pen Jo... what are you doing? Oh.. my.. god... JOOO... wait! wait! NO! NO! NO! NOOO! JO! THIS IS MADNESS!"

[Loud screams as in deep horrible pain; stumbling sound; scraping sound as if nails against the wall; furniture moving; screams following each other rapidly in a maddening crescendo! ...silence ...long anguishing silence ...soft indistinguishable murmuring and whining ...short faint screech in the distance...]

Dr. G: "Jo... Jo... can you hear me..."
JG: "Doc?"
Dr. G: "Jo... Jo... thank god... are you okay?"
JG: "Doc?... where... where am I?"
Dr. G: "Yes it's me Jo, how do you feel... can you... JO!"

[Some sound of movement and furniture moving; rapid breathing; short faint crescendo screech in the distance]

JG: "Doc!! We have to do something... you probably don't understand... it's all clear to me now... I... I must..."

[Sound as if a body falls to the ground; faint but sharp short screech in distance]

Dr. G: "Jo... you have been under a terrible ordeal... I had to hypnotize you to reach deep into your sub conscience Jo.... but this... this is not what I expected... you're bleeding profusely! Jo... we must stop the bleeding... we must get you to a hospital."

JG: "No time for that doc... horrible things are happening... atrocities are about to be committed... why am I bleeding this much doc?"

Dr. G: "You have just stuck a pen all the way up your nose and retrieved something Jo... You then stuck it into your navel and again got a strange thing out of your bowels... we must leave now to get medical help!"

JG: "They did terrible things to me doc... listen... I'm bleeding, but I have to tell you this NOW doc before it may be too late... people have to know doc... help me stem the bleeding and let me finish my story... how long has it been since doc?"

Dr. G: "Months Jo... here press this on your nose... use this one on your navel."

JG: "The dogs doc... the dogs got to me first... I looked over a boulder and saw 'it' hovering... just a feet or 2 above the ground... people were staring as in a trance, but not all of them... I swear I saw a government minister and a few other powerful people... well known people in the community... pushing and shoving those few who were in trance.... then... then 'They' came out... huge hangar like door opened... 'They' were towering beings... human like in body, but their heads... their heads were like beasts! Jackals... hawks... something that looked like a ram... and another one... the biggest one... probably their leader... it had the head of an indescribable beast!"

[Faint, short, sharp screech in the distance]

JG: "They started to grab the poor folks in trance... the others screamed as in terrible fear, but only those in trance were taken... the others stepped back, fell on their knees begging and bowing... It was then that I screamed... some of 'them' looked up in my direction... one of the Jackal headed monstrosities grunted something... and then the dogs came... like a huge swarm... howling in the wind... I tried to run but it was in vain... they surrounded me in no time..."

Dr. G: "Let me help you to this chair Jo... how do you feel... can you manage?"

JG: "Let me finish doc... please.... I... I can manage... you must pay attention... the dogs howled like mad beasts while their masters took me away. I was taken to that strange hovering craft... the dogs have all but disappeared back to where ever they came from that ship... I screamed my lungs out but there was no one else but these strange beings... [heavy breathing] all others either left or were kept in that vehicle... I struggled vigorously but their strength was incredible... they grunted to each other in some strange language... making clicking sounds... sharp dissonant screeches followed by deep grunts or barks, depending on which 'animal' spoke... they brought some sort of metal box and opened it... one of them held my head... I screamed my lungs out when I felt a sharp pain entering my bowels from the back! [Frantic hurtful heavy breathing] ...there was an indescribable painful thrust into my belly and with indescribable panic I saw a huge claw approaching my nose with something metallic in it... I screamed until I could not utter a sound... just a hissing gurgling as bubbles of air left my throat... the agony... the blind maniacal panic... my eyes popped as I saw all surroundings melt into one painful blinding white light... that... that's all I can remember..."

[Sharp, short, clearly audible screech]

Dr. G: "Did you hear that? Did you hear that strange noise?"

JG: "Yes... it came from near your desk... but that sound... that sound... oh my god doc! Those... those things you said I pulled out... where are they?"

Dr. G: "I found one here Jo! There must be one more... here it is! They must have rolled away in all the commotion... Jesus Christ... they're all covered in blood..."

JG: "Let me have a look doc."

[Sharp, short, clearly audible screech; sounds of metal objects falling on the ground]

Dr. G: "Holy shit! Ouch! Did you see that Jo? It gave me a shock! Damn that hurts!"

JG: "There they are doc! Be careful..."

Dr. G: "I'm not going to hold them in may
bare hands again... let me use this cloth...
wait! One of them starts to blink!"
JG: "Both are now blinking doc!!"

[Sharp, short, clearly audible screech]

Dr. G: "Shit!! I... I... think they may have
been monitoring you... us... all this time
Jo... I wonder if these things may explain
your sharp increase in psychic abilities...
who knows, oh my God, I wonder if..."
JG: "Doc be careful! One of them changed
color!"

[Sharp, short, clearly audible screeches
increasing in amplitude in a rapid
crescendo; indescribable short and hard
sound as if a huge gob of goo has been thrown
unto the wall; series of indistinguishable
bursts of white noise mixed with sounds of
some sort of dripping substance; silence...
blank recording]

It is with heavy heart that I managed to put these transcript pieces together. My fingers are absolutely cramped as I tried as best as I can to describe the sounds I heard on these recordings, which are truly indescribable; at moments even unspeakable or unimaginable. What was that last explosive burst sounding like a huge "BLAB!", like a tremendous short circuit had occurred at a high voltage substation... I have no idea... no words to describe the million thoughts racing through my mind. My poor father... what terrible ordeal became his fate?

But no time is available now. I must hurry and deliver this to the authorities. For the last half hour I have had this terrible ominous feeling something dreadful will happen to me. This may sound ludicrous but *I can feel them!* Don't ask me how or why... but the strange noises in the last half hour or so has had a paralyzing grip on me... the howling in the distance, oh my God those faint and yet clearly distinguishable screeching noises... short clatters in the dark... I hope someone may still read my handwriting which has become more erratic every hour. What time is it now? Four, five in the morning? Something is at the door... I write hastily and then try to hide this in time... something is at the door... I fear the unthinkable, therefore I must finish... there! There is a screech at the door!

❈ ❈ ❈ ❈

Postface

   'There are many truths, which are useless for the vulgar to know...'
   Many centuries ago, those have been the words of Marcus Terentius Varro, a Roman scholar. Now, the same thoughts occupied officer Tromp's head while he stood around noon in the windy plains below the hill of Alto Vista. He has been hanging around for almost an hour already, although that didn't bother him so much, as he truly enjoyed the spectacular view of the robust rocky coastline battered constantly by the majestic waves in their endless battle to reclaim land. Wave after wave were producing impressive explosions of white salty clouds of foam each time they fiercely pounded the volcanic rocks. He examined some of the

small towers of wishing stones built by tourists through their years of visiting the island. Suddenly, a small dust cloud in the distant horizon due west caught his attention. A silhouette of probably a jeep was becoming discernible. It was indeed a brown colored rental jeep approaching rapidly. A man and a woman were visible inside. Tourists, probably a couple on their honeymoon, as was usual in this time of year.

The jeep stopped abruptly a few feet next to Tromp.

"Hi there," the man said, "is this the road to baby beach?"

"No. You're terribly lost I'm afraid."

"Are you able to please help us out maybe?"

"I have a map with me."

"A brown colored map?"

"Well yes... actually I have just that."

The man stepped out of the jeep and walked towards Tromp, while he took off the brown backpack he was carrying. They looked at each other silently for a few seconds. All the pre-arranged questions and counter answers were made correctly, and yet, Tromp hesitantly handed out the backpack.

"Is it all here?" the man asked.

"Everything. All transcripts and digital recordings."

"So there is no other hard evidence left to this case?"

"To my knowledge no."

The man put out his hand and said, "well thank you." Tromp shivered as he distinguished a faint sub tone in the man's voice, like a dim subdued screech. Tromp trembled even more when he shook the man's hand, which felt eerily cold and yet strong, causing Tromp hastily to let go of the man's hand and to take a step backwards.

"We have a deal right?" Tromp murmured.

"Absolutely," the man said in a subdued voice. "It will be all there in the offshore account. Thank you again."

There it was! That ominous subdued screech again... just briefly... just a faint undertone... yet nevertheless hearable. Tromp slowly took another step backwards.

"Well thank you again for your map," the man said in a loud voice, turned around, stepped into the jeep, and drove off from where they came.

Tromp just stood there for a while. With a focused gaze, he carefully scanned his surroundings in a 360 degrees sweep. All seemed clear. *They* were gone.

He checked the towers of wishing stones again. To most these seemed like foolish pastimes of tourists on vacation, however to those few initiated by *Them*, some of these were clear bearing marks to the next event.

Tromp started walking towards the direction of the chapel. It will take him another half hour or so to reach his car. He occasionally stopped and looked around... scanning again, trying to detect anything that would confirm the uneasy feeling he had inside. Wasn't that a short faint screech that caught his ear? Unable to see anything suspicious, he would start walking again, feeling somewhat relieved that he just may have been a little to paranoid.

Unbeknownst to Tromp however, for the last 10 minutes, a hairy canine creature had been following him at a distance with steadfastly strides, focusing only on staying out of sight while rapidly diminishing the space between *It* and Tromp.

Unmistakably, one of the few remaining sentinels of outpost Alto Vista...

THE END.

Mehr Licht! (More Light!)

The last words of Johann Wolfgang von Goethe.
(28 August, 1749 – March 22, 1832)
German poet, playwright, novelist, and scientist.

The Leiden Sleep Project

Dossier 1.

"*It*" all started when I met Professor van Veen, a notorious cognitive psychologist from Leiden University. We met unexpectedly at an informal social gathering in café '*het Buitenbeentje*' in Tilburg, where at that time I was lecturing a few courses in Psychology. I use the word *it* on purpose, as there is no logical and rational way to explain the unspeakable events that happened after that first meeting. A bit under influence of my favorite Belgian beer, *Corsendonk Agnus*, I thought at first that the whole topic of our casual conversation was a joke; a relaxed verbal exploration of the outskirts of reality. I was wrong. I was very wrong. I was soon to discover that some doors in our universe were indeed not meant to be opened by the human mind... ever!

You see, I'm a man of science. I believe firmly that the truth, the universal truth, the absolute truth, has to be upheld at all times, and every effort has to be made to discover what lies beyond our horizon of what is acknowledged to be real and true. I write this now in order to prevent others to make the same arrogant mistake van Veen and I have made while upholding our scientific beliefs. There is not much time left before *it* may perhaps have a final abominable conclusion, so I will try to make this as understandable and comprehensible as possible for you, my unsuspecting dear reader... my innocent layman, or perhaps, if I'm fortunate enough, a fellow scientist, who one day may solve this enigma and prevent the darkest of truths to cross over, and reach our side. It's so ironic indeed. In our unquenchable thirst for scientific knowledge, van Veen and I may have started something that still baffles any comprehension and encompasses an archaic threat to humankind for which in all honesty, we, or anybody else for that matter, could have never been prepared for. But first let me go back to that regrettable night at Tilburg which now, in hindsight, I wish could be undone somehow.

The seminar we were all attending that week has somewhat become famous throughout the world as the "Beyond The Bend Conference", a seminar exploring the latest discoveries in the field of psychology, and more specifically, the remote and unexplored borders between cognitive psychology and parapsychology. These seminars were allegedly the cutting edge of neuroscience where some claim the paranormal is meeting our current understanding of physical reality. Forgive me reader if once in a while the terms get technical, but there is no other way to describe this new and fascinating, yet immensely fear instilling branch of science. The title of the seminar was chosen to illustrate what we all felt at that time: that there was a horizon, a bend or curve in our understanding of the universe, where we still were unable to look beyond, and yet we all could *feel something was out there.* Also, we not only hoped, but we all were pretty sure *that something* would soon make its presence be felt. Like I, van Veen had also discovered a clue, an indication, that there may be a way to get in touch with what lies beyond the reach of our known physical senses. Everyone knew Professor van Veen's reputation as a radical, somewhat eccentric, but highly respected scientist. Everyone had a little envy of his bold approaches and courage to stand up to the arrogance of the established scientific community, and his fearless ways of defending his observations. More than once he had defied their skepticism and proven himself right. There are statistical valid indications that the human mind is able, and is perceiving, signals, sights, and sounds from an existing reality beyond our own. The context of this is still highly enigmatic, and may consist of perhaps another dimension, perhaps the results of Quantum Entanglement[2] theory, the so called *"spooky action at a distance"*, or perhaps the proof physicists were waiting for their highly speculative dark matter theory. Whatever it was, van Veen convinced me that night he had discovered a key to unlock that dreadful door...

I can still feel the looks of envy everybody gave me when van Veen approached me that night at the bar of café *'t Buitenbeentje*. I was flattered. You don't get to approach van Veen, he approaches you, and that always created that "chosen one" feeling everybody else was so anxious for. The crème de la crème in the scientific community was present, but van Veen ignored them all and settled next to me at the bar and in his known bold way opened conversation.

"A very intriguing and interesting paper you have published... had to read it twice, but still... very intriguing."

I didn't react on purpose. Instead I slowly took a sip of my *Corsendonk*, reached into my jacket to get a cigarette, lit it up, leisurely turned to my right where he was standing inches away, and said: "Excuse me... do we know each other?"

The guy standing on my left abruptly spurted his scotch onto the bar. Van Veen looked over my shoulder at him, smiled, and extended his right hand out to me.

"I like that..." he said in a casual tone, "Professor Valentijn van Veen, *'triplé Vé'* as my friends call me, Leiden University, Psychology Faculty, intrigued and enchanted to make your acquaintance Mr..."

I shook his hand as firmly as possible. Alpha male style.

---

[2] Quantum Entanglement Theory suggests that certain quantum particles are connected to, and influencing, each other by mysterious pathways in disregard the distance between the two of them. Physicists at Delft University of Technology in the Netherlands, have recently managed to scale up entanglement to engineered objects barely visible to the naked eye.

"Jacobo Ambrosio Cornelio Krozendijk PhD, Tilburg University, Psychology Faculty... but you can call me by my initials... JACK... everybody does so."

I had to smile a bit. He held my hand firmly. "Splendid!" he said, "Splendid indeed! Looks like it's going to be a splendid night after all. Please allow me to buy you another one, you're almost empty."

We took the beer and sat at a quiet corner in the outside terrace. A colleague of mine followed us and tried to make use of the fact that we knew each other to mingle with van Veen.

"Fuck off," van Veen said before the poor man even had a chance to utter a word. There he stood, right hand stretched, about to introduce himself. He looked at me begging for help.

"Are you deaf?" van Veen stood up. "This is a private conversation... so please... fuck... off!"

I looked at him a little uncomfortably and said "I'm sorry Hendrik, I apologize, but this is indeed a very private conversation... maybe at another occasion... truly sorry about this amigo."

van Veen sat back. "Can you believe these kiss-asses?" he asked clearly upset. "What is it with these *'chupadonan'* (suck-ups) anyway? God. By the way, my accent is a little rusty, but do you mind if we continue our conversation in *Papiamento*?[3]"

"Can you speak *Papiamento*? I was under the impression that —"

"As you may well know, my father is Dutch," he interrupted me, "but my mother is from Curacao, albeit from Dutch descendance. Although I'm born and raised here in Holland, she never let me forget her native tongue." He chuckled. "Came in

---

[3] Dutch Antilles Creole Language, with origins in Portuguese, Spanish, Dutch, English, West African, and Arawak. Spoken mainly only in Aruba, Curacao, and Bonaire.

very handy when she and I had to say things not meant for my father's ears," he continued in *Papiamento*.

I had to laugh out loud. Indeed I knew many details of van Veen's general bio, including the background of his parents, but I somehow didn't expect him to be quite fluent in *Papiamento*.

"Well, well," I said choking, "who would have thought of that. A half *macamba*[4] and an Aruban about to conspire how to get beyond the bend."

"Hmm... imagine that... usually a *hodido*[5] combination, but this time I have a good feeling about this."

"Yes indeed...," I continued laughingly, "you people are still holding a grudge against us obtaining our *Status Aparte*[6], but with the years you'll get used to it and learn to stand on your own. No more tax money flowing to your pockets."

"Don't press your luck *Buchi*[7], you forget I'm not really a true *yiu di Korsow*[8], I wasn't born and raised there. Now let's get down to business, shall we, before I change my mind about all of this."

"Wow! ... Slow down amigo!" I rebutted. "Nobody is putting a knife at your throat. You're the one who invited me, remember?"

I patted him on his shoulder. Eyebrows were being raised by those watching us while pretending not to be watching us. van Veen also noticed that and started laughing out loud.

---

[4]Originally a Creole word to denominate a foreigner. Later this word became on the Antilles common to refer to Dutch people, like the word "Gringo" in Spanish to refer to Americans.

[5] Fucked up

[6] In 1986 Aruba separated from the rest of the Netherland Antilles to become an independent member of the Dutch Kingdom.

[7] A common nickname in Aruba, also used to denote an uneducated lower class person.

[8] A Curacao colloquialism to denote someone was born in Curacao; therefore being a *child of Curacao*.

"Jesus," he screamed still laughing, "you're really milking this for what it's worth, aren't you?"

I moved in closer and said "Okay... enough teasing... let's have it... what is it you want to talk about."

"Have you really established contact?" he asked abruptly in the most serious of tones.

"I'm not sure what you mean..."

He came forward and whispered "Come on guy... the case you describe in your paper... the little Afghan girl whose dream sequence you studied so extensively."

"Oh that one," I said affirmably. "Yes I think so. Definitely there was something there... a contact as you name it was in my opinion definitely established... with what? I have no idea, but it was there... *something*... *something unknown* was there doing *I don't know what* to that child's brain."

Van Veen leaned back. He sipped his beer thoughtfully, as if million thoughts were racing through his brain at the same time. The Basima[9] case, as documented in my paper, has indeed created tons of controversy among the psychology community. Nevertheless, the figures are there, and the facts as witnessed by me and various of my colleagues do not lie. Van Veen looked back at me in a most unsettling way. I, on the other hand, looked at him in a puzzled way, still trying to figure out what this controversial persona was up to.

---

[9]Basima was a little 6 year old Afghan girl who came to the Netherlands as a refugee. Her dream cycle and sequences were extensively studied. While in the deepest part of her sleep, she would frequently open her eyes and start describing landscapes, buildings, monuments, often using languages which were most certainly unknown to her. Recordings show her on one occasion even speaking *Papiamento*. She sometimes used a language which up to today no linguistic institute could trace. Statistical analysis showed that it definitely is a language and not the garbled invention of a six year old. Through all these different languages, translated by certified translators, her descriptions of valleys, trenches, buildings etcetera remained consistent. She often referred to them as the house of *Yhor*, the magnificent, the conductor, he who permeates it all.

"How many times and how long have you established this contact?" he asked me in a intense voice. "What I mean is, how many times and for how long each time were you absolutely sure there was *something*?"

"It's all there in my manuscript," I replied. "Every session of it. Every transcript of a possible sure *contact* or *connection*. Problem always was that these contacts didn't last more than a few minutes. It happened only in her deep sleep cycle. Her rapid eye movements during those cycles were astonishing! I have never witnessed something like that before. She was definitely staring at a lot of *things*, and her descriptions were always consistent with her previous episodes. We have pieced a lot of her descriptions together, and it matches no known landscape, monument, building, area, whatsoever known to mankind. We have had a team of archeologists and architects on this... nothing! I mean the mere scale of the described buildings and monuments defies anything built up to now known to man. I know my paper has been scolded, looked down on, and received with skepticism by many peers, but nevertheless, the statements are completely true as witnessed by me and my assistants and colleagues. Statistically it has a 99% significance! And still many of these *pendewnan*[10] still think I have sucked all this out of my thumb!"

"I know what you mean, welcome to my world," van Veen sighed.

He leaned forward while looking around conspicuously. "I think I have found a way of extending that most crucial deep sleep period. I am on to something, but I can't trust anyone," he whispered while clutching my arms. "No one, except my loyal assistant... and probably you. I know I don't know you, and yet after reading your impressive paper on the Basima case, and after witnessing how you stood tall against all those in the scientific

---

[10] *Pendew, pendewnan* (plural). Rude word in *Papiamento* to denote a complete moron.

world that scolded and ridiculed you, my gut feeling tells me I can trust you and that probably only you may be able to understand what I'm up to, and most probably help me dominate *It* when the time is there. You have studied sleep cycles as no one else in this field. I think, no I'm positive, I have the key to unlock the mind's potential... to open it up to unknown and extended perceptions... but for that...," he looked around again and whispered even more softly "you *have* to come with me to my secret lab in Leiden... only there... together... we will unlock this mystery!"

Van Veen took something out of his pocket and showed it to me in the most secretive of ways. It was a tiny flask containing a violet fluorescent liquid.

"This is my latest formula," he whispered, "I'm convinced this time I will get much farther than all previous attempts, but for that I need your help... I need your understanding of sleep sequences and dream interpretation. I have come very far my friend and time is running short. I need to start now before it's too late!"

I took a long, very long look at him. He leaned back while putting the flask away in his jacket, and looked uneasily back and forth at me and at his surroundings, like a paranoid schizophrenic would do when suspecting a conspiracy of the whole world against him. All of a sudden I couldn't hold back anymore. I started to laugh incessantly and hysterically. I screamed while tears were squirting in all directions. He looked at me in absolute bewilderment.

"This is a joke right?" I blurted out. "An elaborate prank," I slapped my knee while laughing hysterically. "Now I get it! They... somebody... they got you into this to ridicule my paper or something like that, isn't?"

I couldn't stop. Wave after wave of laughter emerged from deep within. Van Veen came forward and grabbed my arm violently. His eyes were wide and filled with uncontrollable panic.

"*Coño di bo mama[11]*," he whispered intensely in my face while shaking me fiercely. "Stop that. Somebody's life is here at stake. Stop that!"

He raised his arm about to slap me. I stopped abruptly. A sudden, numbing silence fell on the terrace. Everybody was staring at us. It was as if a giant snapshot had been taken of the whole place. People were frozen in time, some with their glasses raised in midair on their way to take a sip, others with cigarettes in similar positions. A few were just with their mouth open, baffled in disbelief at what they were witnessing. I stared at him, first in disbelief, but gradually with increased realization and awareness that this is bloody serious to him.

"I think it's time for us to leave this place," I said calmly. I grabbed his arm while standing up, and gently pulled him out of his chair. His face was expressionless and seemed to have aged within a few minutes. I looked around until I saw Henk, one of my students, who worked here part time as a barkeeper. I made a gesture to him with my index finger, indicating to put everything on my tab, and that I will be back on a later date to pay. We left immediately and strolled silently in the direction of *Heuvel*, the town's central plaza, where we stopped in front of the *Heuvelse Kerk*, the iconic neo-gothic church building and probably the most famous landmark of Tilburg. It was there and then, facing those odd shaped medieval twin towers of the *Heuvelse Kerk*, that I made that most fatal decision. Why I did it, even when my gut feeling was screaming at me to run as fast away as possible? Curiosity. That unstoppable urge that drives the true scientist. That feeling that you're about to lift a cloak and reveal secrets hidden by eons.

---

[11] Extremely offensive insult in *Papiamento*, involving one's mother

You go on, even when your instincts tell you these enigmas were not meant to be revealed to mankind. That anxious feeling indicating that finally, that most forbidden of all fruits, is within reach...

"Let's head back to Leiden," I whispered to him. "We can go by your hotel and check out, go by my house, grab a few of my things, and head straight to your place in Leiden. It will be only a hour and a half drive. I'll take a good look first thing at whatever it is you are asking of me and make my decision there. I promise that in the case I refuse to help you, I will not reveal anything I hear or see. You have my word as a professional on this."

He looked me straight in the eyes, took a deep breath afterwards, and silently shook my hand. It was there and then that I felt that creepy ominous feeling all too well familiar to us all... that tight knot deep in your belly warning you that somebody was going to get hurt real bad.

※ ※ ※ ※

Dossier 2.

The drive to Leiden was made in complete silence. Neither van Veen or I felt like talking, each of us submerged in our own thoughts. That quietness came somewhat as a relief after our episode at the café. After about an hour and a half, while reaching the outskirts of Leiden, van Veen broke silence.

"Take the route to downtown."

"I know where the faculty is, I —"

"We're not going to the faculty," he interrupted softly. "My lab isn't situated there... you will understand when we get there."

I nodded quietly and followed instructions. It was almost midnight when we arrived at an old building at a quay of the Nieuwe Rijn, downtown Leiden. My first impression was that this was an odd place for a psychology lab, but then again, it did seem the kind of place where you would like to conduct secret experiments, avoiding prying eyes and sensitive ears. My suspicion seemed correct. While descending into the basement through a long winding staircase, I noted that all the walls were covered in foam and egg boxes. The kind you find in cheap recording studios. After what seemed an endless descent into the bowels of this old house, we reached a steel door. van Veen knocked 3 times... then 2... then 4 times. The door opened and we were greeted by a spiffy looking young fellow with the looks of too much caffeine, too late at night.

After settling down, van Veen made the formal introduction.

"Professor Krozendijk, meet my most trusted assistant and graduate student drs.[12] Albert Schoonhuizen. Albert, Professor

---

[12] Short for doctorandus, the Dutch title equivalent to Master of Science.

Krozendijk here is from Tilburg University, Psychology Faculty... uh... is it all right he calls you Jack?"

I nodded and shook Albert's hand. "My pleasure," I said.

"Well okay then... Albert, Jack here is unaware of our project and experiments, but before I give him a complete briefing, let's quickly go through our daily routine test. It has been two days since I left for the seminar, so we have some catching up to do. How did everything go during my absence?"

"The usual," Albert replied. "Nothing strange or out of the normal to report."

"Very well, let's start. Jack, could you please sit here and watch us go through the test?"

We all sat down around a table and van Veen immediately started to ask Albert all sorts of questions. Mathematical questions, general knowledge questions like what was the capital of Japan, personal questions about Albert's past, etcetera. I was kind of puzzled at first but then realized that this seemed somewhat familiar to me as a sort of cognitive test, the type of test one would take to observe mental alertness, indications of Alzheimer, or perhaps the degree of a subject's sleep deprivation. After the questions, van Veen proceeded with a standard array of tests to check Albert's reaction speed. He seemed satisfied when finished.

"Very well... now Albert, if you will excuse us, Jack and I will head to the meeting room where I can brief him about our project here. Can you please arrange for some coffee?"

"How would you like your coffee sir?" Albert asked me.

"Black, no cream, no sugar please."

"Very well, you guys go ahead, I will bring it to you."

We left the room and I was amazed at the size of this underground complex. There was a corridor with various doors on each side, and it all struck me as like those compounds you see in spy movies, where government agents work in all secrecy, or covert villains plan how to take over the world. This was totally unexpected. Baffling I might add.

Van Veen looked over his shoulder while walking, and smirked "Impressive, isn't it?"

"Mmm-hm," I nodded.

"All this was built during the second world war, right under the noses of the Gestapo," van Veen explained. "The family who owned the house kept entire Jewish families here, and planned numerous raids against the German occupying forces. It's amazing indeed how they managed to get away with all this."

He stopped at a door, opened it and said "This is where you will sleep and live while staying here, if you decide to join us."

He then proceeded to another door, opened it, made a grand gesture and said "Welcome to our brainstorming den. Here is where evil plans are made," he said with an evil laugh, clearly intended as a pun.

Although I was still overwhelmed, I had to laugh too. The room was again bigger than expected, with cabinets on the side, and a large conference table in the center. We sat face to face at one of the corners.

There was a moment of silence. Perhaps van Veen had to order his thoughts or try to figure out how best to start explaining. I myself was glad for the brief pause. [There was] still so much to process mentally, although I had an ominous feeling I was embracing just the tip of the iceberg.

"How much do you know that really happens inside the mind when asleep?" he started.

"Not sure what you mean... much is still a mystery."

"Let me be more specific and cut to the chase," he interrupted. "Much of the existing scientific community refuses to accept valid statistical data indicating that during sleep, specifically deep sleep cycles, the human mind is able to open up and perceive an array of signals it does not seem to identify while conscious. Meanwhile, the indications that this is indeed happening are increasingly overwhelming with each new study. The Basima case in your recent report may well be the apex of all reported cases. I mean, the statistical data and analysis you presented is so strong that it has shaken the scientific community, even although most of it pretends that nothing has happened. However, please don't take this as a reproach. You have not presented a single hypothesis that may be the source providing the mind with these signals, or what the possible mental processes may be which are obtaining these impressions."

"Yes, but —"

"And I understand perfectly," he cut me off. "You did not want to speculate and fuel the hordes of skeptics out there. You just wanted to present the facts with enough evidence that they must abide by it, and then start the inevitable scientific discussion and speculation. Am I right?"

"Yes, indeed you are."

"Well, based on my own studies and experiments I have come up with an idea of what maybe happening... but please, first, let me hear what you think is going on, I'm sure you must have come up with something."

I felt a bit uneasy, shifted my position in the chair a few times, and then decided to fire away anyhow. I felt I finally found the right set of ears to listen to my ideas, which I might add, seemed sometimes outrageous even to me.

"Something is out there..." I started. "Something is definitely out there, and it is trying to communicate. It is trying to reach out to us. The strongest indication I have that this must be the case was with Basima. If the mind opens up during deep sleep and receives random signals, and with signals I mean all sorts of sensory input like images, sounds, smells and tastes from all sorts of places, then you would have a clear scattered array of unrelated perceptions. However, besides the usual garbled *'noise'* the mind seemed to pick up during those brief moments of deep sleep, many of my earlier subjects indicated a high incidence of more or less the same type of input or perception. And that was the bottleneck. Signals were only noticeable during deep sleep periods, which normally lasted a minute at the most. However Basima... whew! Basima somehow stayed longer in contact, sometimes up to 5 minutes, and her signals were much, much more consistent with those of her previous sleep periods. It seemed that she was almost always going to the same *place* and talking with the same *something* that was out there. Besides that, to make things even more astonishing, during her episodes Basima could speak in languages she could never ever have learned. Swahili, German, Aboriginal dialects to name a few, I mean, she even spoke *Papiamento* once. It was as if *something* with far more knowledge and insights took over her mind, and tried to control it. Of course many explanations are possible, but let me tell you, my observations and analysis constantly brings me to the same conclusion... *something is out there trying to communicate!*"

Van Veen let out a deep sigh. "I'm not going to argue with you or speculate on what you said. There is just not enough time for that. You'll understand in a minute." He took out the little flask with the violet fluorescent liquid, and placed it in front of me.

"I have come to somewhat the same line of thought as you," he said, "and I too think that the bottleneck to further development is the fact that the deep sleep cycle is too brief. We all know that deep sleep cycles usually can last up to 100 minutes. So why are these subjects experiencing such short deep sleep periods? Why can't they maintain a normal deep sleep cycle like anybody else?"

"Hmmm," I murmured. "Good question, although I cannot provide definite proof based on statistics at this point, my gut feeling tells me they try to fight or avoid *something* that is happening to them during deep sleep."

"Exactly!" van Veen exclaimed. "Exactly!... My God! How come no one else sees this? Are we the only ones mad enough to acknowledge these observations, or are all the rest of them stupid or afraid to consider this?"

van Veen pointed vigorously to the tiny flask in the middle of the table.

"What if I tell you that I came up with a possible solution to our bottleneck problem?"

"You have definitely got my complete attention by now, don't you think? Please continue," I said with some humor.

"You see Jack, at first I tried everything in my knowledge to prolong the subject's deep sleep periods. I used all sorts of drugs to induce sleep. To no avail. They just slept longer, but their deep sleep cycles remained unusually short. Worse than that, during those few moments of deep sleep they were unable to relay the signals they perceived. They were simply too numb to speak, although it was evident that they were perceiving signals and fighting them as vigorously as before."

He paused briefly and leaned forward.

"So I went the other way around," he said with twinkling eyes.

"How so? I inquired. "How do you mean?"

Before he could answer, Albert came in with a tray containing coffee, two cups, some cream and sugar with a few cookies on the side.

"It took a bit longer than usual, sorry about that," he said, "but I had to finish my report to be sure to include all details." He placed the tray in front of us. "Anything else?" he asked.

"No thanks, very kind of you," van Veen replied. "Oh by the way, there may be something. Can you tell me exactly on what day October the first, 2024, will fall?"

Albert smiled. "Still trying to catch me aren't you?" he said with a little laughter, "it will fall on a Tuesday."

"Damn you're good!" van Veen replied with joy, "Damn good indeed."

"Now gentleman," Albert said, "if you'll excuse me I have to attend to a few other things, so I'll leave you to your affairs for now. Anything else, please don't hesitate to ask."

"Thank you," I said. "Most kind of you."

After Albert left, van Veen leaned forward and said, "What do you think of him?"

"How do you mean, in what aspect?"

"I mean how does he come over to you. Does he seem alert, like sound of mind, intelligent, normal, etcetera?" van Veen inquired anxiously.

"Well so far yes," I said with a laugh. "Normal... attentive... intelligent... even a bit savant considering the recent stunt he just pulled with the date. But tell me, and forgive me if I'm wrong, why do I get the impression that you seem to constantly test him for his cognitive abilities?"

"*Eynan e rabo di porco ta krul mi amigo,*"[13] van Veen said with a deep sigh while leaning backwards.

---

[13] An old saying in Papiamento. Literally it means "that's where the pig's tail starts to curl, indicating that that's where the real problem(s) begins.

He took a long look at me. My heartbeat went up, as an eerie silence permeated the room. *'Here it comes...'* an inner voice whispered in my head, *'...here it comes. La revelación.'*

van Veen finally broke the suffocating silence.

"You see... Albert here," he said in a strange voice, "...Albert hasn't had a minute sleep for the last 20 days."

❖ ❖ ❖ ❖

Dossier 3.

There comes a time in the life of every man of science, and I mean the true scientist at heart, where he starts to question the purpose of his existence, the meaning of his work as a contribution to mankind, the necessity of his sacrifices, the ethics of his chosen methods, and whether or not his discoveries and achievements one day will reach immortality. Every passionate man of science says he will do anything if he is certain that his actions will bring him the understanding of what lies beyond the horizon of human knowledge and understanding; yet, only those who have been at that crossroad can comprehend the total despair encountered when facing the uncertainty about choices to be made, and their probable catastrophic consequences, not only for themselves and loved ones, but perhaps even for mankind in its totality.

All these thoughts were racing through my mind while I was pacing through the room, like a tiger in its cage. Should I thank them for the opportunity and leave this insane situation, or should I grab this chance to unveil what seems to be an archaic mystery of the human mind. What if we were about to unlock doors not meant to be opened by the human mind; what if we were about to open that which has been closed upon humankind on purpose eons ago... what if... what if. How gruesome these torturing inner doubts were, I can not deny what I have seen and heard during my time with Basima. My "gestalt" has been tarnished, corrupted; tainted by sounds and sights which challenge all logical foundations of human perception. I stood at the end of the room with my back to van Veen, facing an empty wall while my mind projected biblical visions of the forbidden fruit and that first fatal bite which condemned humanity out of paradise. Resistance was futile I realized... the dice were about to be cast... once again.

I turned around and looked at van Veen who has been sitting there patiently all along, awaiting the result of my inner struggle. He had been there himself. He gazed at a folder in front of him, avoiding any eye contact as not to influence my final decision.

"I am ready," I said.

He looked at me now.

"Sure?" he asked.

"Positive," I sighed. "Come on let's have it". I walked back to the table and sat on my chair.

Van Veen pointed at the little flask with the violet fluorescent liquid.

"This is *ZetadiCabannoidChloride*... I call it 'Potion Z'... it's made from two mysterious plants found in the heart of Zaire, and was brought to my attention by a Belgian roommate of mine during my time as an intern in Leuven. He grew up in Zaire, while his father functioned there as a biologist for the Tropical Institute of Brussels, and brought the plants with him when he came to live back in Belgium. When the leaves of both plants are blended in the right proportion and chewed upon, they create a curious state of complete alertness while suppressing sleep and fatigue for quite some time. Arno, my Belgian roommate, and I used to consume this mixture right before exam periods. We would stay awake for about a week and achieve astonishing learning capabilities. Unfortunately, no matter how much you chewed, after 7 to 10 days, the inevitable crash would occur and you would fall into a deep sleep lasting a day or two."

I grabbed the small flask and took a closer look at its content.

"I assume you somehow managed to synthesize a stronger blend?" I asked.

"Indeed," he replied. "Not only that, but I managed to work out a dosage that seems to keep you going for days in a row."

Van Veen took a deep breath.

"In fact," he continued, "I have no idea for how long this formula will keep you on your feet. Let me explain it this way... one drop of this elixir will last you about a little more than a day. So each morning, Albert takes exactly one drop. He has been doing so for the last 20 days, without any noticeable side effect."

Van Veen opened the folder and showed me a picture of what seemed to be a bunch of rodents.

"These are the fantastic four," he said with a tender smile. "They were my first subjects I tried my formula on."

I looked at the picture wondering why he was showing me four white rats staring playfully into the camera. He then showed me a second picture of the same 'fantastic four'. Not only weren't they looking so fantastic anymore, the sheer horror of it took me totally by surprise. I couldn't help but just gasp for air as I was struggling not to throw up right there and then. Where there once have been playful eyes there existed only gruesome charred black holes. There teeth had grown absurdly large, and their lovely white color had changed into an shocking filthy shade of grey.

Van Veen looked at both pictures with somewhat sad eyes.

"The first picture," he said, "was right after they have taken the first dose. They stayed playing and frolicking for two whole days, and at the first signs that the effect was starting to wear out I gave them a second dose, and so on, until I managed for them to stay awake and joyful for a full week."

He sighed. "Then...," he continued while he blinked away a small tear, "the unimaginable... the unthinkable... happened totally unexpected. As expected they crashed into a deep sleep which I somehow anticipated to last about a day or two, three, to the most. The second picture shows the result of that sleep. You see, the whole idea was to prove that after artificially being kept awake, they would fall in such a deep sleep that hopefully they would resist for a while whatever stimuli would try to wake them up. Just long enough so I could monitor their brain activity and check for any unusual outside interference. Instead, within two days they changed into these abominations. They never woke up, but it was clear that they were involved in a furious subconscious battle with... with... I don't know... *something!*"

"What do you mean exactly..."

"Well... it was apparent that within hours something extreme was taking place. They started to wriggle and contort in the most horrible ways. They would randomly open their eyes and scream in what seemed unbearable pain, their voices sometimes in such a high pitch that only instruments could register it. At those moments they would just stare in the distance with their mouths open to maximum capacity and their tongues rigidly sticking out. The instruments would indicate extreme loud and high pitch sounds which of course the human ear was unable to capture. Here, let me show you."

Van Veen took a remote control and pointed it to a stereo set.

"I have recorded most of it and managed to digitally alter the pitch to lower it to human levels. Please listen to this. I must warn you though... it will not be pleasant!"

There is no way van Veen could have warned me for what was to come. At the first sound waves, I was instantly rocked from my chair, fell to my knees and started to vomit violently. I waved frantically in the air with my right arm while holding as strong as possible to my belly with my left arm. Wave after wave of vomit came with each subsequent brutal noise-burst leaving the tortured speaker system. Before van Veen could react and shut things down, I crapped all over myself and passed out.

❖ ❖ ❖ ❖

Dossier 4.

I woke up in a different room, lying on a couch, wearing clean clothes and smelling fresh. There was a small table in front of the couch and at the other side were two lounge chairs with van Veen and Albert each sitting in one of them. My head felt somewhat dizzy, punch drunk maybe, as I tried to sit up. Albert stood up and offered me a hand. He then got back to his own chair and we all remained silent for a while. I stared confused at them, they stared back with an expression that the worst was yet to come. It was then that I noticed there was another one of those folders on van Veen's lap.

Van Veen broke silence. "I am truly sorry for what happened. Your reaction was much stronger than anticipated and none of us had any idea that such a averse response was even possible. Nevertheless, I must ask you if you think you feel up to it to continue right now. Time is running short. Are you okay?"

I rubbed my face briskly with two hands and murmured a subdued "Yes."

"Are you up to continuing?"

I nodded okay.

"Very well. Allow me to finish explaining what happened to the rats. Within about 36 hours of intense struggle with whatever they had encountered in their deep sleep, all four rats grew extremely violent as in a huge subconscious rage. Technically they were still asleep, but physically they withered away fast... their eyes sunk to dark bottomless pits... their teeth grew in grotesque proportions while their skeleton contorted under extreme pains, with blood oozing out of their skin where bones seemed to be snapping internally to splinters. Their skin and fur turned to a sickening ash grey, and they soon died violently and suddenly, as if whatever they were dealing with abruptly lost all interest and left. You see... they should have been dead within a few hours after their deep sleep struggle started, but they were being kept alive by *something*... as if being *zombiefied* ...*as if an external force was controlling their physical parts!*"

I looked in bewilderment at Albert. He nodded in agreement. Actually, I didn't know if he was nodding to reaffirm what van Veen was stating or that he was nodding as an answer to my expression of bafflement and which I think was showing my thoughts... my God Albert... *are you realizing what is going to happen to you once you stop taking this potion?*

Van Veen answered instead. "If it is what I think you're thinking, than the answer is yes. We are fully aware what we have put ourselves into and that's why we must proceed rapidly and urge you to focus, as time is running out quickly. And yes," van Veen raised his hand in a gesture to interrupt me what I was to say, "I know that I'm not the one at risk here, but that nevertheless does not make things less serious."

Albert took the folder from van Veen's lap and opened it. The first page was the picture of a cute chimpanzee. "Oh my god...," I whispered as I braced myself emotionally for what was obviously to come.

"Jack," Albert said, "this here is Bono. A two year old chimp, and our next test subject. After the rat incident we chose to follow up straight ahead with a subject psychologically much closer to our own species. We had a hypothesis of what occurred to the rats, and we needed a mentally and physically stronger subject... unfortunately... things didn't go well for Bono also."

He showed me the second page. I stood up in shock, completely horrified, instantly disoriented by the gruesome manner Bono's body was contorted and the insanity of what must have happened to accomplish such horrific remains. Above all the portrayed madness, what instantly struck me were Bono's eyes, what remained from them. Two dark bottomless holes with an eerie amorphous structure, from which no light seemed capable to reflect, and that nevertheless seemed to stare inexplicably straight at you. Maybe it was the macabre ensemble of a gasping mouth with horrifying alien teeth arranged in such an unholy way, accompanied by a mashed formless nose, which somehow seemed to guide your gaze straight to those dark spiraling entrances to the inner core of what must have been an abominable otherworldly soul. I was eyes wide open, staring in horror, yet also in blasphemous fascination, at what must have been the expression of an incredible, unimaginable, powerful, outer dimensional monstrous creature. I stood there... frozen. Nothing on this earth will ever match this 'what the fuck' moment!

Albert and van Veen all of a sudden started to laugh insanely. They were screaming their head off in hysterical insane maniacal laughter. Albert threw the rest of the folder up in the air and yelled as a freshman on spring break, while van Veen threw himself on the ground laughing uncontrollably. I just stood there in total disorientation... like someone that went over joyously to collect the mega million lottery price, and was being told that the numbers were correct, but the date is from last year's draw.

"I... I... Oh... oh... ooooh... now... now I get it...," I started to stutter, "...it's a prank right? I... I was right after all, right? It's a goddamn sick prank... RIGHT?"

Surprisingly, I just fell back on the couch and started to laugh as well. Soon the whole room was reverberating with our insane laughter. I was crying and laughing at the same time. What an emotional ride this has been! Van Veen stumbled still laughing towards a cabinet and took a bottle of Glenlivet single malt out of it, uncorked it and took a huge sip from it before passing it to Albert, who on his turn looked at the bottle, looked at van Veen, and started to laugh even harder than before. "You son of a bitch!" he screamed laughingly at van Veen, "You know I can't drink this!"

Albert shoved me the bottle and sat down next to me, still giggling and coughing from all the laughing. Both van Veen and Albert seemed to be calming down as well, and were breathing exhausted; exhaling their last laughs. The room started to fill with silence as all hilarity seemed to fade away.

"Jesus Christ you mother..."

Van Veen instantly cut me short with one simple hand movement.

"It's not a joke", he said in a serious tone contrasting all previous amusement.

Albert stood up and placed a hand on my shoulder.

"It's not a joke Jack... we just had to laugh. We just had to relieve this immense pressure that has been building up all these months... somehow your face... when you saw Bono's last picture... I mean... by God that picture packs a punch. Somehow your face just broke the dam and made us laugh at the insanity of it all. Please, allow me to fill you in with some details."

Albert sat next to me and continued.

"Do you know what happens when you're asleep Jack? Besides all theories and hypotheses, do you really know what happens? Never mind the electronics, the scans, the graphs. Do you have any idea what goes on in your brain the moment you fall asleep?"

I must admit Albert had me there. Indeed, all the scientific world had were theories, suspicions, hypotheses, but not much else. We know long lasting memories are supposed to be formed. New neurological pathways are probably being created. But exasperatingly little is known for sure. On top of all these scientific conjectures, we are now facing a totally new mystery. Both van Veen's and my own experiment clearly show that there might be *something* out there trying to communicate, trying to reach out perhaps, and it does this only when subjects are asleep. We also suspect that only a few possess the ability to perceive this entity or force. Without going into too much scientific jargon, I must concur somehow with a most interesting concept Albert and van Veen explained to me that night. Something I have only suspected, but up to that moment haven't given the attention it deserved: *That during sleep, and specially during deep sleep periods, the brain opens up channels and capabilities of perceptions not present when awake. In our dreams we unintentionally or unknowingly open up channels and portals through which other beings may access, perhaps control, our very essence, and we unsuspectingly enter or contact other dimensions. Some sort of intertwinement of neurological pathways, perhaps an unknown sort of synesthesia![14]*

While Albert and van Veen continued their dissertation into their fascinating hypothesis, I stood up and started to pace the room. This was a new and most disturbing probable aspect of reality! Imagine the staggering consequences if unchecked and out of control. While innocently asleep, otherworldly horrors may have access to the unsuspecting mind. God knows to what purpose! We yet have trouble accepting and understanding contemporary science, and now it may be most likely that what theoretical mathematicians and physicists have conjectured on paper may be true after all. The existence of other dimensions! Most likely, inhabited by creatures unimaginable to us... the mere thought made me shiver with horror. Ask yourself this dear reader, bear with these most uncanny thoughts... do you know what happens inside your brain while you're asleep? Let's be totally honest and objective. Most of the eight hours or so we sleep are a total black abyss, except for a few dreams here and there, a complete physical and spiritual oblivion. The more I jumbled these concepts around in my mind, the more I became aware that this was indeed fascinating beyond imagination! This could explain many of the weird phenomena human kind has experienced

---

[14] Synesthesia, a genetically linked neuropsychological trait in which the stimulation of one sense causes the automatic experience of another sense.
This phenomenon affects 2 to 5 percent of the general population (source: ENCYCLOPÆDIA BRITANNICA)

throughout the ages. Clairvoyance... déjà vu... dreamscapes... spiritual conveyances... my God! The possibilities seemed endless!

I started to understand the whole concept behind van Veen's experiment, how ludicrous, bizarre, and hideous it may seem. After so many days without sleep, Albert is to sink into a vast deep sleep, and as a virtual cerebral speleologist try to explore a dark bottomless subconscious cave, holding on to that deep sleep as long as humanly possible to extract whatever ultra dimensional secrets that mental abyss may hold. The possible outcome of such insane experiment was evident in the pictures shown to me, and yet, to the true man of science, one who has the capabilities to shut down all human emotion and abhorrence towards the most outrageous experiments envisioned to push the outskirts of human understanding of reality, this insane and preposterous setup made complete sense. Oh yes... hold on to your heart, my dear layman, as we hardcore scientists indeed are willing to bargain with the devil himself if it provides a glimpse of what lies beyond our horizon of understanding... even if that bargain may cost us our sanity in the end! Yes we know that there is a chance the human mind is not meant to encompass all of the universe's secrets, and yes, by God, we are fully aware that we may be intellectually marooned on a tiny island of consciousness, engulfed by an immense dark sea of secrets for which we are most likely incapable to ever design a suitable mental vessel to cross its cosmic vastness. We as a species are most likely only doomed to drown in that infinite ocean of incomprehensible enigmas. And yet, nevertheless, the lure of knowing it all one day is the only essence worth living for in the eyes of a true man of science. To quote Proust: *"The only real voyage of discovery consists not in seeking new landscapes but in having new eyes"*. Here, in these hidden dungeons at Leiden, we were about to create new eyes. May God have mercy on our souls for what we are about to undertake!

❖ ❖ ❖ ❖

Dossier 5.

How to best describe the events that happened the next few days is beyond any words known to mankind. How does one describe the indescribable? What words can you come up with when looking into a new dimension of pain, suffering, trauma, and personal hell? If you've just opened a portal to a new dimension, how do you create new words for things incomprehensible to the human mind? I will try my best dear reader, with the meager vocabulary left to me after having stared cosmic horror in the eyes.

After about one day of not taking the elixir, Albert soon started to fall in a semi trance state of mind. Sleep was clearly trying to take over, but as soon as Albert dozed off and shut his eyes he would soon wake up screaming in panic. He would then looked confused, as if trying to recognize where he was, and then would rapidly start to tell us what had just spooked him in these short instant nightmares. All of these narrations were of course recorded on tape for future reference.

Albert told of quick succeeding visions of brutal landscapes, interspersed by what seemed gigantic cities of an unknown architecture. Winds were howling constantly, he said, and an immense feeling of desolation could be felt everywhere. It wasn't a planet or such, his impression was, but more of a cosmic structure, something permeating vast areas of another universe. Sometimes Albert would shake vigorously in fear, as he stated that *They* were soon about to discover him. What *They* were, he could not tell, but he sensed them everywhere and *They* were hunting him down. Soon he would keep quiet, and with increased frequency and intensity, he would start to doze off again. Soon afterwards, we confined him in a specially designed room. It was the last time I spoke Albert in his regular human form.

Albert was now in a very deep sleep. Van Veen had administered him some sort of a truth serum, and switched on all the monitoring systems installed in the room. Albert's body was by now hooked up to all sorts of instruments. Van Veen stated that the only thing left to do now was to wait. The truth serum was a new twist to the experiment, van Veen added, it would hopefully allow Albert to remain in control longer of his senses and give him the ability to communicate in a coherent way as long as possible before *the phenomenon,* as van Veen called it, would finally take possession. I listened to all this with increased fascination on how well this whole experiment was thought through.

After all set, van Veen and I sat in the monitoring room next to the lab. There was a long and anxious moment of silence before van Veen all of a sudden spoke again.

"You know, I should have been the one lying there," he said.

"How so? I thought it's the assistant's task to do all the dirty jobs."

"Sarcasm suits you well young Skywalker[15]...the emperor will be pleased."

I had to laugh. "Okay smartass, tell me, why are you not lying in there instead of him."

"He made me toss a coin," van Veen sighed. "Otherwise all deals were off and I would have had to find me another assistant, and trust me, there is no replacement for someone like Albert. True

---

[15] Luke Skywalker, a character from the Star Wars saga

committed scientists are extremely hard to find these days. Lots of wannabe's out there who just want to share the limelight, but when it comes to taking risks and stepping into unchartered waters, they all crawl back under their rock. Not him. He just produced a coin and insisted the winner would be the 'lucky' one. At the end I have this feeling that he always would have ended there anyway. Both of us knew that I am better prepared to carry things on."

Van Veen paused a while, and then with a puzzled look he said "I want you to listen to this... see what you can make out of it. Please come with me."

He took me back to the conference room, and placed a tape into the cassette recorder.

"Please listen to this," he said, "it's a recording of Bono's session. Don't be afraid. You will not get sick again ... well, not as sick as the first time anyway."

My body stiffened as he pressed the play button. There were faint moaning, which crescendoed to screams and gasps. There was no doubt these were made by a chimp, but all of a sudden, the sounds produced, changed in articulation. The hysterical pitch remained the same, but there was this verbal aspect slowly permeating into it.

"By God!" I exclaimed. "It's... it's... it's trying to say something, isn't it?... It's trying to speak!"

"Yep," van Veen affirmed. "Listen carefully now... here it comes..."

Only the background hum could be heard now from the cassette player.

"Y...H...O...R," came out crackling abruptly out of the speakers.   "Y-H-O-R...   YHORRRRR... GGRRRYOOOHHHRRR..."

"Holy shit!" I gasped. "But this is impossible! Chimps lack the necessary vocal structure to do this! How... how..."

"He was being forced to... physically manipulated if you will, to produce these sounds. It was there at that point that the gruesome changes started to occur on its face."

Van Veen abruptly switched off the cassette player. Sounds could be heard coming out of the observation lab through the intercom speakers. While we rushed back to the monitoring room, van Veen explained that Bono managed to produce more incredible sounds just before his face and body were mangled into that indescribable abomination observed in the photograph. The whole ordeal lasted only a few minutes he said.

Albert was awake, or so it seemed. A strange gaze into an unknown distance dominated his face. The result of a trance like state I presumed. Van Veen took us straight into the lab. We were standing on both sides of the bed where Albert had been securely strapped on. Van Veen started carefully.

"Albert... do you hear me... what do you see Albert."

"Its immensity... it stretches far beyond our imagination. ...It breathes ... the signs on the wall ...they were here before!"

Albert started to wave his hand in a strange manner, which seemed like a signal to me.

"Quick! Hand me that piece of paper!" van Veen shouted. I complied hastily. Van Veen loosened Albert's arm a bit and placed the paper under his hand and a pencil in it. Albert scribbled in a hasty way unreadable symbols, and then dropped the pencil. Van Veen instantly tightened the belt again fixing Albert's arm and hand firm to the bed. I picked up the paper and looked at it. It made no immediate sense to me.

"They were here before," Albert whispered.

"How do you know that Albert," van Veen asked.

"I just know... I can feel it... I can feel *Them* ... they know I'm here... with T*hem*... I'm still, but my consciousness seems to expand and encompass it all. I can see it all! The plains are enormous, the desolation total, and the temperatures vary extremely! There are huge mountains, higher than anything we've ever seen, and amidst the vast valleys in between are cities scattered everywhere, populated with monstrous buildings containing incredible domes topped by monolithic pillars so high they seem to disappear into dark skies; yet at their top I can see they have starfish like heads, each with a giant eye in the centre and tentacles protruding at each extremity. Far away, at the edge of an immensely distant horizon, I notice gigantic pyramids, their bases as large as continents! These beings, I cannot clearly distinguish their physical form, but their presence can be felt humming inside these structures, these pyramids, these abhorrent dome like protrusions reaching to black star studded skies. I'm hiding ... I must hide."

Albert was sweating profusely. His whole face was showing intense fear, yet his gaze remained transfixed to a point somewhere in infinity.

"*They* were here before... Aaaargh... I can feel my consciousness expanding like a bubble in infinite vacuum... *They* were here eons before us... *They are the ancient ones!*"

Albert's eyes widened to impossible proportions.

"They want to get back! They want what they have once possessed! They want what they have lost! It's a portal! They wander through the mind of those susceptible as they are innocently asleep. Lurking in their psyche ...searching for a way to transcend into our realm!"

Van Veen looked frantically at the monitors, which were showing graphs spiking in all sorts of directions. The intensity of the beeps and blips were accelerating rapidly. He quickly reached out and opened a valve at one of the intravenous tubes as wide as possible, while hastily shouting "Quick! Pass me the ice-cloth!"

I was petrified.

"Don't just stand there you idiot!" he screamed at me. "Move!"

I just couldn't! There is no excuse, no explanation, I was just in a shock like state, overwhelmed by this unholy experience and the torrent of abominable thoughts it evoked in my mind.

"Tell us about the portal Albert!" van Veen screamed. "Quick! What is it you see... what are you —"

Albert suddenly shivered violently all over his body.

"There!" he screamed. "I can see what the tentacles are for! They are reaching to us while we are asleep! I can see thousands of us lying in a peaceful slumber... unaware that they are being probed by archaic forces far more ancient than imaginable! These beings... they are manipulating our psyche as if trying to break a code, as if rotating the opening mechanism of a spiritual safe... They want what they once had! Control! Total control! They are incessantly trying to create a portal to transgress into our dimension. We are in great danger... my God... we are in extreme danger!"

Albert twisted violently again. The monitoring devices were going haywire, and some indicators were just flying out of bounds! His contorted body was drenched in sweat as he started to scream hysterically "Ooohhh... OOOOHHH! I can feel *Him*... their conductor, the magnificent one, he who permeates it all, he who commands the black goat with a thousand kids... *YHOOOORRR!"*

Albert let out the most unbearable horrible scream I've ever heard in my life! With a hideous sound his left jawbone snapped like a twig splashing blood all over the place. His eyeballs swelled even more while his skull started to deform and elongate into monstrous starfish like proportions.

"Yalehgr! Rlyatorg muscat!" he screamed in incomprehensible sounds. His tongue took grotesque proportions in his mouth while slowly rows of grotesque teeth were starting to protrude from his fractured jawbone. With a deafening crack his ribs cave in only to bounce back to pierce his skin. His legs started to contort into bizarre shapes. He turned his face to van Veen and made an incredible effort to make his next words comprehensible.

"Q..Q..Quick... Yoouuu ...m-m-must c-c-lose ...c..close ...the g...g...gate. You ...m-m-m-muuuus-stttt c-c-close it now!"

His whole body unexpectedly twisted around its axis an incredible 180 degrees, while his head still remained fixed at van Veen. Albert let out an incredible scream while his eyes started to expand even further! The breath he let out with that scream filled the whole room with a hideous stench. I couldn't help but shit myself again in disbelief. His face started to turn away from van Veen as he began to scream incessantly while seemingly fighting with all his strength at whatever power was trying to force his face into another direction.

"Yalehgr. Yhor muscat. YHOOORRR org muscat! Aresh! Areshga! Areshrrrgaaaaa!"

"BANG! BANG! BANG!"

Totally unexpected and with incredible speed van Veen produced a gun and shot Albert square in the face! The sound ripped my eardrums apart and its echoes carried all through the room for quite some time. Albert's body twisted and shook violently until all was quiet. A faint whistling sound started to swell in my ears as I looked confused at the whole bizarre scene.

There was blood everywhere. Albert's horrendous, starfish-shaped face had exploded as a watermelon, leaving a big gaping hole filled with grotesquely shaped teeth. Van Veen just stood there, his arm holding the gun bungling at his side, while he held his forehead with his other hand. His face had an absurd and strange look of disbelief. He turned his face slowly to me and stared at me with an expression as if asking for forgiveness. He raised his gun to the side of his head, and before I could have uttered a sound, he shot himself dead. I just stood there for God knows how long... mute... deaf... confused; with my soul shred to countless pieces...

❖ ❖ ❖ ❖

Epilogue

Bear with me dear reader, whether you are a fellow man of science, a miserable excuse of a scientist, or an innocent layman, but the accounts you just read describe the incredible and horrific events as they happened 25 years ago at Leiden. Yes indeed, 25 long years have passed since I have plunged myself into this scientific nightmare, and in the mean time, the world has changed in many ways thanks to huge technological advancements, which, I must admit, I once thought could only exist as fantasies in the deranged minds of science-fiction writers. Regrettably, I too became greedy in my unquenchable thirst for knowledge, and I confess, with heavy heart, that I have conducted unspeakable experiments on unsuspecting beings in that secret underground lab. Collateral damage I have whispered many times, trying to appease my conscience after another horrible death had occurred. But, if any consolation, all was not in vain as I have come to some remarkable observations! I can not prove my suspicions entirely, but I have the strong impression that as a species we're slowly slipping into a dark abyss, as if these horrendous beings Albert pointed out are progressively gaining in their hideous intentions; dragging us deeper into uncharted depths. The recent phoenix-like rise of dark ideologies, and their elevation of terrorism to yet unknown heights, strongly concur with my earlier predictions that sinister forces are getting a stronger hold on a larger collective consciousness. On the surface it just may seem as if mankind will never learn and that what happened eons ago will just continue to happen again in the near future, but is this really the case? Are we the *only* masters of our own fate, or are there, as Albert suggested, *others* with a more disturbing interest in us; secretly attempting to create strings with which to manipulate us like puppets.

With time, of which as you'll soon understand, I had more than my fair share, a horrifying concept started to emerge. It all became clear to me with the rise of computer technology and the internet. Just like hackers use the net to infiltrate unprotected computers, what if these entities as witnessed by Albert, can access susceptible innocent minds in their sleep and manipulate these at will? What if these beings are trying relentlessly to find a way to enter our dimension and take possession to what they claim to be rightfully theirs? I tell you my friend... definite proof still eludes me, but my keen instinct developed over hundreds of thousands of hours of experimentation and observation tells me that this is exactly what's happening. Human minds are gradually and collectively being infused with unspeakable horrors and affected by glimpses of realms not meant to be witnessed by the human soul.

Unfortunately, my time is nearly over. As you perhaps may have suspected dear reader, as a true man of science I too couldn't resist the temptation of going beyond the bend, to try to take a peek at what lies past our horizon of knowledge; to dip my feet into that vast ocean of cosmic mysteries where we just float around as insignificant beings. I went on a search and found van Veen's stash of that fascinating elixir that glows so preciously in the dark. I took my first drop of potion 'Z' a few days after the horrific climax of the Leiden sleep project. My senses became incredibly sharp, and for two hundred and nineteen thousand hours without a single second of sleep, my mind raced all that time through countless ideas and possibilities, creating and discarding endless amounts of hypotheses concerning our species, our creation, and our place in the universe.

It's a shame that all good things must come to an end. I have only a few drops left. Soon I will tumble into a much dreaded sleep that will take me to terrifying horrors, for which I fear, I yet have no adequate response. It all depends now whether my mind has evolved through all these years into an organ capable to cope with that vast ocean of cosmic secrets and mysteries.

However, to you my friend, my dear reader, I can only issue words of caution... *beware of your sleep!* Mark these warning words dear reader, as I cannot emphasize them enough! As the Dutch say, *'een gewaarschuwd man telt voor twee'* (forewarned is forearmed). Monitor and record your sleep with every technological means possible. Watch and listen carefully to those tapes you record. Look for unexpected contortions. Listen vigilantly to the sounds you make. Between those innocent sounding snores you may detect a conspicuous mumble of incomprehensible syllables. Unknowingly, you may be one of those accessed by *Them*! For now you can still close your eyes hoping for the best, but soon, in a few days, my eyes will have to close, and the outcome of my unwanted sleep is definitely unknown and most certainly to be feared. I sincerely regret that, like Eve, I too couldn't resist to bite in the forbidden fruit of knowledge. May God forgive my sins, and have mercy on us all!

The End.

Never spit upwards. It may fall on your face.

Old Arubian proverb.

Karma

1. An undesired discovery

For way too long, silence has been a blanket in which I have comfortably draped myself with to cover many secrets. However, the recent discovery of new details about the truly disturbing disappearance of my dearest uncle Dr. Mobuto 41 years ago, has turned previous uncertainty and speculations into a horrifying reality of unimaginable proportions, for which I can no longer remain silent. Let this document be my final catharsis, as for what I'm about to reveal will have a far fetching impact on the human psyche. But, before I cause sleepless nights to those able to understand what I'm about to imply in this testament, please let me provide you, my dear reader, with the necessary background information to comprehend the scope of my recent discovery and its horrifying implications to humankind.

My name is Alex Nobrega and I grew up in the small town of Tanki Flip, Aruba, a tiny island pertaining to the Kingdom of the Netherlands, and innocently floating on the Caribbean sea a few miles north of Venezuela. My father, the late George Nobrega, a hard working carpenter with a humble education and straight as an arrow morals, died when I was very young. My mother, Maria Eckmeyer, was a school teacher who sacrificed her youth so I could enjoy the best education both my parents never had. Finally, Esteban Eckmeyer, a.k.a. Dr. Mobuto, Aruba's most famous magician and practitioner of the dark arts, was my mother's only brother, and since the passing away of my father, the only mentor and male role model I knew as a child. He lived next door, in a simple house, which never revealed neither his financial wellbeing nor his phenomenal status as a world class magician. He would travel the world for months many times on his grand tours, but there was one thing we all could be sure about: Dr. Mobuto would never miss a Christmas with his family. Until, that is, that fateful Christmas in 1972. I was then only 12 years of age.

Dr. Mobuto would always arrive back on the island around the 15th of December. His daughter Selma and I would already be waiting anxiously for the past few days for whatever marvels he would bring from the four corners of the earth. He would not only shower us with gifts and exotic curiosa, but also with the most fascinating stories about his adventures in strange and remote places. Indian Maharajas, European Royalty, African Kings and South American dictators, all would bow to the mysteries and enigmas presented to them by the strange Dr. Mobuto, master of the underworld and lord of the linking rings. In those days, without the luxury of the internet and modern communication technology, news would travel slow, and a man could easily get lost in his own backyard for days without being able to reach for help. So to us, the fact that by the 20th of December he had not showed up without prior notice wasn't that disturbing at all. We just wondered and grew more anxious to all the goodies he would bring. In our infantile imagination, he was just busy collecting more gifts and thus was having some delay arranging proper transportation of it all to the tiny island of Aruba, but by the time Christmas has passed and the new year was on our doorsteps, my mother started to show serious signs of distress and preoccupation. "This was very unlike him," she would often say, and she was sure something serious had happened.

That year we had the saddest holiday season in our life. While on the 31st of December at midnight the whole island dutifully burned a few million dollars in fireworks – a tradition brought here by Chinese immigrants at the beginning of the century – we instead were sitting quietly in the living room staring at the beautifully adorned Christmas tree. At its trunk, the presents bought for my uncle lay unopened since Christmas. My mother often would cry silently, something she did with increased frequency for the last days. She was indeed inconsolable. To us it seemed Dr. Mobuto, master of the underworld and lord of the linking rings, had been swallowed by the earth. I was to discover much later that we were not far at that time from the real horrifying truth.

By the 6th of January, the day the Catholic Church celebrates the epiphany of the Lord, Three Kings Day, or as we say in Papiamento *"Tres Reyes"*, my mother went to the police and declared my uncle officially as missing. No telegram, no phone call, no letter, no sign whatsoever, this was so, so unusual for my uncle she stated to the police. She was convinced something terrible had happened, she could feel it in her bones. Now that the authorities became involved, the wait for news, and its inherent tension, became unbearable. However, the first clue that indeed something terrible had happened to my uncle didn't come from the local authorities, but from Alberto "Buchi" van der Linden, a local fisherman used to navigate the coastal waters of nearby Venezuela. Three days after my mother started the official investigation, Buchi arrived at Savaneta, a well known fisherman's village in Aruba, with a faded piece of a local Venezuelan newspaper named *"El Gavilán de Coro"* (The Hawk from Coro). He went straight to our house to show my mother the ominous article on page 15 about the mysterious disappearance of a famous Aruban magician. The translated article read as follows:

Moruy, Falcon State - In the remote small village of Moruy at the foot of Mount St. Anna, rumors abound that a man from the nearby island of Aruba, together with other local individuals, have disappeared under mysterious circumstances. The man in question was staying as a guest at the remote shack of a local character known to the villagers as *El Chamán* (the Shaman), a notorious practitioner of witchcraft and the dark arts. Local authorities from Punto Fijo are investigating the allegations from the villagers that on the night of the 31st of December, *El Chamán* together with the Aruban, which by now the locals were calling *El Mago* (the Magician), were seen heading with other unknown individuals to the top of Mount St. Anna, which at that time was shrouded by thick clouds emanating an eerie violet color, supposedly due to a heavy electric storm at the top. Authorities are still searching the whole of Mount St. Anna, but up to now no trace whatsoever of the small group has yet been found. Authorities are considering the possibility that this strange group of men obviously associated with the darker arts, may have been murdered by a mob of local superstitious villagers, and that the whole Mount St. Anna story may be a cover up. However, most testimonies considered reliable by the authorities indicate that perhaps indeed something terrible has happened at the summit of Mount St. Anna. Chief of police at Punto Fijo, Mr. Jorge Echevería, recognized the Aruban man on a photograph (see above), taken a few days before at the town square by an inquisitive local, as world famous magician internationally known by the alias Dr. Mobuto. We will keep you informed of future developments of this strange case.

This article came as a sledgehammer blow to us all. My mother sank into her chair and wept uncontrollably while Selma and I wandered confused and with tears in our eyes for what seemed hours through the streets of Tanki Flip. Soon, everyone in the neighborhood surrounded my house and offered their condolences to my mother and tried to console her in whatever way possible. It goes without saying that this was the saddest day of our lives. Or so I thought at that time ...

❧ ❧ ❧ ❧

As the days passed, and more and more news reached us through official channels, we reconciled with the fact that Dr. Mobuto may never lighten up our Christmas seasons again. His body was never found, neither at Mount St. Anna, nor anywhere else in the state of Falcón, or elsewhere in the world for that matter. My mother remained inconsolable and never recuperated from that terrible blow. For Selma and I, life slowly went back to normal. Selma moved that same terrible day to our house and lived with us until she went to study in Florida. Dr. Mobuto's house never became abandoned. My mother would open it every morning and perform the necessary chores to maintain it. She insisted the house remained intact, and we all knew her reason for doing so: her silent hope that one day he may return. Selma and I would tend to the few doves and rabbits that remained, until the day they passed away through natural causes.

Sometimes, mostly in the afternoon, when the rays of the setting sun would create beams of surreal wonders through the blinds, I would go over to my uncle's house and sit in the grand couch in the living room. In solitude I would breathe in the majestic atmosphere of mystery that was always present there. It was the only room that conveyed the vastness of Dr. Mobuto's world travels and adventures. Wall to wall shelves with books proceeding from all parts of the world covering all sorts of topics. A huge tiger hide covered the center of the room. Strange instruments would adorn the cabinet at the far side, and in the middle of it, a huge bell jar would show the head of a notorious Papua New Guinea warrior, supposedly killed by the own hands of Dr. Mobuto while pursuing my uncle's own cranium as a trophy. He always said how that single defining moment in time, that fierce struggle in the remote jungles of Papua New Guinea, has changed his perception of life forever.

"The taking of a man's life, my son," he often used to say at the end, "is an omnipotent feeling of power, infused as a venom into your soul. That defining moment you realize that it is going to be him and not you that will leave this earth, is a maddening sensation creating unholy pleasures of might through your whole body. Avoid having to come to that at all times my boy, as it will change your whole perception of life forever, and will dull your senses in appreciating the beauty in the simple things of being alive."

Those words would often ring in my head, but I never could really understand them. Until, that is, I discovered a darker side I never ever knew nor suspected of my beloved uncle Dr. Mobuto, master of the underworld and lord of the linking rings.

You see, dear reader, I really did love my uncle with all my heart. He was, and in a strange way still is, the most charming and caring man I have ever met. Always a kind word when it came to appraising one's efforts, and when it came to one's failures or mischievous deeds, never a harsh reprimand without a suitable explanation why and how to improve oneself. Always producing a small gift in a magical way on the most unexpected moments, just to cheer you up on a rainy day. He immensely loved his daughter, his only sister and me. After his disappearance, and after he was declared legally dead by the authorities, his testament showed he had left his vast financial recourses to my mother, to be managed entirely until Selma became of age, until which she would automatically inherit half of it. I truly loved and admired him with all my heart, until that fateful day I decided to open a door which perhaps I should have never opened...

❖ ❖ ❖ ❖

At the age of 18, I graduated from *Colegio Arubano*, the highest form of high school education here in Aruba. I finished cum laude at the highest curriculum available at *Colegio*, which was ASE, Advanced Scientific Education. An achievement, for which I will be eternally grateful to my mother, who sacrificed youth and beauty, never to remarry or engage in casual affairs with other men, with the sole purpose to relentlessly guide Selma and I successfully through high school and our pursuit of a professional career abroad. Not an easy task, considering my somewhat adventurous and mischievous character traits as an adolescent. Nevertheless, one day, I found myself at the doorsteps of the prestigious Massachusetts Institute of Technology, where I went to study Electrical Engineering, Computer Science, and Space Aeronautics.

It was during one of my winter breaks on Aruba, that curiosity finally got the upper hand over my mother's strict warning never to open the door to the basement leading to my uncle's private chambers below the house.

"Have some respect for the deceased!" she yelled at me after I repeatedly nagged her about not being allowed to sniff around in the basement. "Good heavens Alex, why can't you understand this issue? Those were his private quarters. If they were meant to be visited by us he would have invited us there a long time ago, don't you think? *Carajo!*[16] What's wrong with you? You're a grown man, 22 years of age, studying God knows all sorts of complicated topics, and you still can't understand such a simple thing? Don't let me ever catch you going there. It is his private room, for God's sake. Besides, that room is creepy as hell, and still scares the living shit out of me."

"You see what I mean?" I protested. "You enter that room all the time to tidy it up, you always tell me how that room creeps you out, you damn well know that all your insinuations about strange things in that room will make me curious as hell, and you still prohibit me to just enter it once at least to see what it looks from the inside."

"*Carajo*, Alex!" she screamed hysterically. "The answer is NO. NO. NO! Stay away from that damned room, God damn it." I could swear I saw some degree of panic in her eyes that afternoon.

I let the issue rest, but not for long. Soon enough one night she went with a few friends to her local pastime, "Mega Bingo" at the Alhambra Casino, located at the low rise Hotel area at the western part of the island, near Eagle Beach, the longest and best beach of Aruba. I knew it would be at least 4 hours before she would be back home, so I decided with a thumping heart to take the keychain and head to my uncle's basement. The lure of finally entering the private quarters of Dr. Mobuto was indeed somewhat intoxicating. I couldn't wait to lay my hand on what could

---

[16] A Spanish expletive attributative.

probably be some of the most exiting secrets gathered from the four corners of the earth.

Upon opening the door I expected to be hit by the stale odor of a room closed the majority of time for over 10 years, but surprisingly enough, the faint stench was bearable. The result of my mother's thorough housekeeping. What hit me visually though upon switching the light was the astonishing beauty of all the woodwork and the neatness of the whole place. The dark tropical bookshelves were full of ancient books, the workbench, equally elaborate in its wood decorations, was polished and shining under the old fashioned Victorian age lamps hanging low from the ceilings, and the wooden floor was just breathtaking. This wasn't only the work of thorough maintenance by my mother, but the painstaking design of a man of the world, with a taste in precious things nourished by years of travel and exploration.

The stark contrast between the yellowish light produced by the lamps, and the dark areas of deep shadow they cast at the far sides of the room, created an eerie gothic atmosphere, the kind that makes you recall the cat and mouse game shadow and light played in movies like Frankenstein or Dracula. There was an uncanny quietness through the whole room, and from where I was standing I could barely see there were two more doors at the far side of the room. I took a deep breath. The air felt heavy, and I felt lost. My God, what an iconic cinematic mystery room this was. Where to start looking? How on earth would I be able to explore most of it in a mere three and a half hours time?

I decided to check out the grand bookshelf first. The books were beautifully made, showing true craftsmanship, and must have cost him a fortune and great effort to collect. Although most titles were at that time abracadabra to me, it was much, much later, that I discovered my uncle possessed one of the largest collection of forbidden literature known to mankind. Knowledge of these book's content carried the risk of horrible impact on the innocent mind, and the abuse thereof could have terrible consequences to the existence of the human race. It was years later that I realized that what at first seemed ancient books about magic and prestidigitation, were in fact no less than notorious works such as the macabre *Necronomicon* by the mad Arab Abdul Alhazred, *De Vermis Mysteriis* by Ludwig Prince, the frightful *Book of Eibon*, the infamous *Cultes des Goules* by the Comte d'Erlette, the enigmatic *Pnakotic Manuscripts*; last but not least, the horrible *Unaussprechlichen Kulten*[17] by the psychotic German philosopher Friedrich von Junzt. By the time I had finished reading these horrible documents containing the most inner secrets of the dark arts, it was way too late. I then realized these codices of infernal facts had slowly but steadily raped my once innocent mind and ripped my soul to shreds. Have I known then what I know now about their hideous and abominable content, I would have most certainly abide by my mother's mandate never to set foot in that room.

While admiring the enormous bookshelf, a small beep at my wrist startled me. I had set my watch's timer to exactly one hour to help me keep track of the time I spend there. I reset the timer for another hour, and proceeded to check his marvelous workbench made from dark tropical wood. It was partly covered with a chemical lab setup, its tubes intertwining like spaghetti and connecting various bottles, Erlenmeyer flasks, and distillation equipment; the content thereof long gone through the process of evaporation. Next to the lab setup were various manila folders containing documents, and what seemed to be a notebook of some

---

[17] Original volumes of these works are all kept currently in a secret vault at the library of the Miskatonic University in Arkham, Massachusetts.

kind. Superficial examination indicated that its content seemed to be a diary, in which he noted his work on the manipulation of animals, especially doves, for the purpose of incorporating them into his stage act. Some entries referred to the manila folders in front of me and upon opening one of them to see what the logbook referred to, I remained in complete shock and horror. It contained detailed pictures of doves that were horribly maimed, body parts of birds that seem to have been dissected, deformed heads, and many more of the sort, all of which too horrific to comprehend at that instance.

A cold wave of terrible fear swept suddenly through my body as I came to realize that these awful pictures may have been from the doves I have cared for so lovingly as a child. It was one of my childhood chores to take care of his aviary, for which he provided me with a handsome allowance. I always wondered though why so many doves seemed to disappear so often, only to be replaced by new ones within a few days. I never asked, as my upbringing taught me it was disrespectful to question grownups, but still, I couldn't help being constantly curious about it.

I looked hastily at my watch. Still two and a half hours left. I realized I couldn't take any of these away with me as my mother would certainly notice this, so I decided to sit down and take as much in as humanly possible in the little time that was left. Feverishly I turned page after page, and slowly the horrific thought began to crystallize in my mind that maybe my sweet charismatic uncle wasn't picture perfect after all. Some of the entries in his diary were so appalling and shocking that I had to resist with all my might not to throw up all over the lab table. What better way to show the content to you, dear reader, than to recite some of these horrible passages, which I'm still able to do after all these years:

...the most difficult part to handle when cutting up a dove to prepare it for performance is the correct adaptation of the sternum bone in a such way that it will reduce the bird's overall size and volume, yet still maintain enough muscular grip to allow it to flap its wings without the ability of flight, and most important, allow the bird to breathe just enough as not to faint or suffocate while in the magician's harness. With enough practice, and the expenditure of hundreds of pigeons, I manage now to obtain a success rate of about 3 out of 4 birds, with about 50 percent of the successful operations producing a minimum survival time span of the doves of 2 to 3 hours, enough to perform one show minimum...

...Yesterday I saw that great Belgian magician Louis de Gryze perform at the Kurhaus in Scheveningen. I was baffled at the tiny harnesses he was able to squeeze some large pigeons into. Nowhere was the slightest bulge detectable in his jacket, and he surprised everyone with some dove productions out of his bare shirt after he had taken off his jacket! His doves even looked a bit spiffier than mine. Obviously he had discovered a better way than mine to further reduce the dove's pain. After the show we met in a party, where after many drinks he whispered in my ear he has finally succeeded in preparing that secret potion he was researching for so many years. The only fact he let slip in his drunken slur was that it was made using indigenous plants found deep inside the jungles of Belgian Congo. The bastard would not give away more details, no matter how many drinks I gave

him. I decided then and there that, by
whatever means necessary, I must obtain his
secret before others do...

Needless to say, the more I read his diary, the more devastated I was by his cruelty and ruthlessness. The diary went on and on about where to cut the poor animals tendons in order to attain a millimeter more flexibility, how to weld cuts and ruptured arteries with hot wax to stem any bleeding, how to cover up wounds by ripping inner feathers and gluing them on outer layers in the right manner to conceal any lesions, and many more unthinkable cruel procedures just to obtain maximum concealment of the birds during stage performance.

A quick glance at my watch showed me there was little than an hour left. I just couldn't risk being found here, so I decided I had enough atrocities by uncle Mobuto, and called it the night. While closing the manila folders, one newspaper cutout fell to the floor, whose headline instantly caught my attention:

FAMOUS BELGIAN MAGICIAN STABBED TO DEATH

Leopoldville, Belgian Congo - The lifeless body of famous Belgian magician Louis de Gryze, a.k.a. *De Vlaemse Fantoom* (see picture), was found dead this morning by personnel of the prestigious hotel *La Gemme du Congo*. Local authorities stated that the deceased has been viciously stabbed numerous times in his sleep, while a dove was being stuffed deep into his throat. Interrogation of security personnel and neighboring guests produced no positive results, as all clues indicate that the perpetrator managed to slip in and out of the guarded compound almost in a ninja like fashion. Based on the statement of René Buytengaerde, Louis de Gryze's close and personal assistant, authorities are now looking for two other magicians for questioning in relation to the mysterious case. One of them is well known German magician Klaus Siegfried von Schwarzkopf, a.k.a. *Die Unglaubliche Blitzgott*, and the other the famous magician from the Caribbean, Esteban Eckmeyer, a.k.a. *Dr. Mobuto*. According to Mr. Buytengaerde, both men had recently issued threats to de Gryze in connection with his refusal to reveal certain of his most intimate magic secrets. Mr. Buytengaerde declared also that both men have been currently seen in the city, which prompted Mr. de Gryze to enhance his own security. Mr. Louis de Gryze was a well known guest and performer here in Leopoldville, and will be dearly missed by all of us. Our most sincere condolences to his family and friends.

++++

BREAKING NEWS! BREAKING NEWS!

At the last minute before closing this edition, local authorities have informed us that the body of well known German magician Klaus Siegfried von Schwarzkopf was found floating lifelessly in the Congo river. A dead pigeon was also found stuffed into his mouth and throat. We will keep you informed of further developments in this gruesome case.

Needless to say I spend the rest of the winter break devastated by the discoveries made with respect to my once beloved uncle. My mother frequently asked me why my sudden loss of appetite and my longing for solitude, but proper words eluded me to explain myself. On the other hand, I must also admit I didn't know how to handle all this and even if I could trust her as before. Has she read those horrible books? If so, has she only read those frightening books, or was she also aware of all his wrongdoings? Was that the reason why she forbid me to enter my uncle's basement dwellings? If she knew, was she condoning all this? If she had not read any book, and if she was not aware of any of his atrocious acts, why then on earth would she prohibit me so fiercely to enter those rooms, only to respect her brother's belongings? I don't know and dared not ask. Soon after, I left heavyhearted back to New England to continue my studies, although this time, as a troubled and saddened young man.

❖ ❖ ❖ ❖

2. An unexpected revelation

It was an unusual cold October night, when I received that fateful phone call from my boss Dr. Heinrich Sauchendaum at the very secretive Institute of Alien Technology at NASA, where I was working for some time on various highly classified projects. I remember waking up in cold sweat as usual, which happened frequently as the result of having recurrent nightmares about the contents of those horrible books from my uncle's library. It was 1997 and still those damned books managed to rave through my psyche. As always, it took about a minute before I realized who and where I was. My wife Angela waited patiently until I was settled before she handed me the phone. I heard the voice of an anxious and frantic Dr. Sauchendaum.

"Alex... You have to come immediately to the center. You have to come now. Tell your wife you don't know when you're coming back. Bring traveling clothes. Pack now and come as quickly as you can. You can shower here at the center. You are leaving first thing in the morning to Aruba." He hung up, and I remained thunderstruck.

It was about an one hour drive from home to the secret center for Alien studies, where the Institute of Alien Technology was situated in Florida. During that lonely drive, I had ample time to allow the wildest speculations roam my mind what on earth had spooked Dr. Sauchendaum in such a manner as to call me in the dead of night. Strange, even weird, how things can turn out in life, I mused in silence. I graduated in 1988 from the Massachusetts Institute of Technology with a Master's degree in Electrical Engineering and a PhD in Computer Science, and because of my extraordinary interests in Space exploration and Astronomy, the National Aeronautics and Space Administration soon showed a high interest in my services. After about two years working there, I was approached by Dr. Sauchendaum to form part of his team working at a secret department of NASA named the Institute of Alien Technology.

Dr. Sauchendaum was a bit of a legend at the department. He was the son of Professor Dr. Gustav Sauchendaum, Obersturmbannführer in the SS, who worked directly under Heinrich Himmler, Reichsführer-SS and founder of the Ahnenerbe Institute, which not only conducted research into the ancestry of the Aryan race, but also in all secrecy in the occult sciences, one of Himmler's obsessions. At the age of 9, young Heinrich Sauchendaum joined the Hitlerjugend and at the age of 16, at the end of the war, he was scurrying the underbelly of Berlin, battling the advancing Soviet troops in a futile attempt to win the war. His father often told him stories about ancient civilizations and occult phenomena, which in time fomented his unusual interest in everything occult and mysterious. After the Nuremberg trials exposed the atrocities of the Waffen-SS, he had an extreme change of heart and became utterly ashamed of what his country had done to humanity. He emigrated to the United States and vowed to help correct the wrongdoings of his generation. His outstanding performance at school won him a scholarship at the Massachusetts Institute of Technology where he graduated with a Master's degree in Aeronautics. A lesser known fact however, is that he also obtained a PhD in Paranormal Studies at the Miskatonic University in Arkham, Massachusetts. When I asked him why he had chosen me to join his team, he just answered with a smile: "You seem to have read some interesting books my boy..."

❖ ❖ ❖ ❖

The atmosphere at the center was frantic to say the least. Four o'clock in the morning and the whole compound was bustling with activity. Something big must have happened indeed. I was immediately escorted to the underground conference room, where Dr. Sauchendaum was standing in front and others were waiting seated at the large table. My impression, that except for Dr. Sauchendaum nobody else present really knew what was going on, proved to be right as soon as I took a seat and all lights went out.

"Dear colleagues," Dr. Sauchendaum immediately started. "The picture you see projected on screen is from the region of Alto Vista on the north coast of the island of Aruba. As you can see it is a rocky and rugged terrain with a chapel on the hilltop, which gives the region its name. Alto Vista in the local language means high or elevated view. Around 2 o'clock in the morning local

Aruban time, 1 o'clock our time, an unknown aircraft, we believe an alien UFO, crashed at these surroundings."

The room exploded instantly with an avalanche of murmurs and anxious whispering.

"PLEASE!" Sauchendaum yelled. "Let's not behave as teenagers. We are professionals." The room soon went quiet.

"Thank you," he continued. "We have immediately been contacted by the Dutch Government in the Hague to assist the local Dutch marine and Aruban authorities in a top secret investigation. Much is yet unknown, but my gut instinct tells me this is it. This is what we have been working and waiting for, for so long. If the pictures sent don't lie, the Roswell incident will be peanuts compared to this. I have selected Alex Nobrega as head of our investigating team. He is a native Aruban, born and raised, and already a respected scientist in our reclusive community. Alex you are leaving in two hours in a military plane to Aruba, I suggest you get ready and report to my office in one hour where you will be briefed in private by General Kim Un Koi and myself."

❈ ❈ ❈ ❈

The flight to Aruba went by military aircraft. We left around seven o'clock in the morning and expected a three hour flight before arriving at Queen Beatrix Airport in Oranjestad. I recall making myself comfortable and let the recent events pass over and over again through my mind.

General Kim Un Koi no less, I thought by myself. If he has been involved into this crisis, I reflected, something serious indeed may be expected. General Kim was a most controversial figure, whose services were reluctantly accepted by NASA at the insistence of Dr. Sauchendaum. General Kim was a high ranking officer in the North Korean Army, who witnessed firsthand the notorious UFO incident at the remote village of Yongha in central North Korea in 1962. He was one of the few survivors of what is considered to be the only violent UFO incident recorded in history. While investigating reports of strange lights and flying objects deep in the rugged mountains north of the Taedong river near Yongha, General Kim and his men suddenly stepped into what seemed to be a secret UFO base. A violent shootout was the result. All UFO's scrambled and disappeared from the area, never reported to have been seen again, while only the General and a few of his men made it alive out of the woods. After the surviving men started to mysteriously disappear one by one, General Kim suspected the involvement of the North Korean regime and defected to the United States. The CIA didn't trust General Kim, as they couldn't make sure where his loyalties were, but at the insistence of Dr. Sauchendaum, the general now resides under close surveillance as a member of the Alien Technology team.

I looked at the manila folder on my lap, which I received from Dr. Sauchendaum while being briefed.

"In there, Alex, you will find everything we know up to now of what just happened in Aruba, and everything you may need to consider to carry out this mission. Please study this carefully on your way to Aruba," Dr. Sauchendaum said upon handing it over. He then paused for a moment and continued softly, "As a young boy in the Hitlerjugend I always had to recite Reichsführer-SS Himmler's words: 'This is a hard job, but if the act is not carried out at once, instead of us exterminating the Jews, the Jews will exterminate the Germans at a later date. We have to stand firm!'... I think the moment has come for humanity to stand firm."

"What the Doctor tries to say is that no alien should be left alive," General Kim followed up, while he stood up from his chair.

"No one. You have to make sure of that. Whatever is found alive over there must be killed at once! Do you understand this?"

Those were harsh words I thought at that moment. Of course I nodded yes, but I most certainly wasn't planning on carrying those orders as if I was a mindless brute. I was a man of science, for crying out loud. General Kim Un Koi may be used to mindless humanoid soldiers following orders blindly, but he got the wrong guy if he thinks I'm going to kill anything before examining it.

Dr. Sauchendaum seemed to sense my inner thoughts. He placed a hand on my arm and spoke softly.

"Do you remember your uncle's library son? You recall the content of those books that to this day still give you nightmares and try to subdue your psyche? How long have you been battling these horrible secrets? Well let me tell you this Alex ... some of us know more about the content of these books than you do. The great Roman scholar Marcus Terentius Varro once said: 'There are many truths which are useless for the vulgar to know, and many falsities which it fits the people should not suppose are falsities'... think about this when you confront the beast."

"Man is simply not ready for what we suspect to be an universal truth," General Kim Un Koi whispered with a grave voice. "Think not only about the chaos this will stir throughout the religious world, but most of all remember Christopher Columbus."

I frowned upon hearing that statement. What are these guys smoking, I thought by myself. What the hell has Columbus to do with all this? I shook my head slightly, as may be the lack of sleep was playing a part in my thinking, because the meaning of all was eluding me at that time. Dr. Sauchendaum stood up and placed a hand on my shoulder.

"Imagine that the first native Caribbean people killed Columbus and his entire crew on first sight. Come on Alex, think about it for a second. Don't you think perhaps the future outcome for them would have been different? Consider that at that time the establishment in Europe thought that the world was flat and that Columbus was crazy. Don't you think the fact that he never came back, disappeared into thin air, fallen of the edge of the world, would have made them think twice about sending another expedition? Would there even be anyone volunteering for such a journey?"

I remember sitting there jaws open. Baffled. Indeed the thought had never occurred to me. Somehow these men had a point, how appalling it may sound to a scientist, they may have a point.

"Wouldn't this not go against our scientific credo Dr. Sauchendaum?" I argued hesitantly. "Aren't we as men of science not obliged to investigate and research new forms of life? Aren't we doing all possible to make the SETI[18] project a success?"

"Aaarrrhg... Those grass smoking fools in California," Dr. Sauchendaum snapped furiously while waving his hands briskly in the air. "Idealists... Dreamers. Echoes from the hippy culture. What are they to expect? Make love not war to aliens?"

"What if these aliens are friendly, loving, intelligent beings?" I snapped back.

"What if they're not?" General Kim Un Koi shouted as he also stood up. I must admit afterwards that from my point of view, sitting in a chair while these two dinosaurs from a distant past were standing angry nearby, was somewhat a frightening, intimidating sight.

---

[18] A nonprofit organization set up in 1984 in California by Thomas Pierson and Dr. Jill Carter. Its mission is to "explore, understand and explain the origin, nature and prevalence of life in the universe". SETI stands for "Search for Extra-Terrestrial Intelligence".

"Answer me Nobrega, WHAT... IF... THEY... ARE... NOT?" the general continued with bloodshot eyes staring right at me. "Wasn't Columbus received with open arms? ... Forgive me my moment of impatience," he said, lowering his voice as he continued. "I forget that indeed you have never stood still at this topic, but think about it for a moment Alex. What was Columbus's definite advantage against the islanders upon arriving?"

I remained silent. Some night this has resulted to be I thought. My God, wake up, went through my mind, this must be a nightmare. God, I felt tired at that moment.

"Wasn't it superior technology?" the general continued in a calmer tone. "Wasn't it the unknown diseases the Caribbean islanders weren't prepared to endure?"

I recall feeling somewhat stupid.

"Yes."

"Do you understand our most grave concern in this matter Alex?" Dr. Sauchendaum asked as he brought me a glass of bourbon on the rocks. I took a sip and nodded my head. God I felt like such a child being lectured at school.

"I changed my mind about Reichsführer-SS Himmler a long time ago Alex, but in the situation we might be finding ourselves now, I must agree with him in one thing ... We must stand firm."

"Not only do we have to stand firm," the general added, "we simply cannot take any chances with a civilization that has managed the technology of interstellar travel. We are the islanders now Alex. It is not us that managed to reach them, it's the other way around. We are at their mercy. It is them that have the power to decide whether to befriend us with 'mirrors and beads' or to finish us off and colonize this planet. We simply cannot take that risk. Do you understand this Alex?"

I sighed. "Ah Yes, whatever," I replied sarcastically.

"You do not sound very convinced Alex," the doctor said in an ominous tone.

"Yes! Yes! YES!" I said raising my voice. "I understand completely. Damn it. This goes against every fabric of my scientific believes, but yes, I understand the risk and what has to be done. *Coño di boso mama ohm.*"

"What? Whose mama?" the general asked in a threatening voice as he turned his head in my direction.

"Never mind asshole," I smirked at him as I stood up from my chair, "You're not in Korea now, so come down that high horse *Chino.*[19]"

There was an intense sense of suspense hanging in the air. The doctor and the general exchanged glances. What's going on here, I wondered for a moment. What's all this 'glance exchanging' all about? The doctor nodded his head briefly, and I could feel the general also relax his posture. I noticed the doctor looked at the general again in a strange manner, as giving him a secret signal. The general nodded, looked back at me and said "Very well, so be it." He waved his hand softly in the direction of the far side of the room. Out of the dark shadows of the corner, a man in military uniform stepped quietly forward, looked at me with an expressionless glance for a moment and then directed his attention to the general.

"This is Colonel Rodriguez. He will be your trigger in this mission so you don't have to soil your pretty office hands with alien blood. He is instructed to deal, and I mean really deal, with whatever possible scenario may occur... and I do mean whatever scenario may occur."

"Oh really?" I whispered. "Wow... have we come to this now."

---

[19] Derogatory word in *Papiamento* used to denote people from East Asian descendance. Like the word 'Chink' in English.

"Colonel Carlos Ramirez Rodriguez is a green beret, Vietnam vet, Iraqi war vet, expert in hand to hand combat, of full unconditional loyalty...," the general paused for a moment, "...and will know how to deal with traitors, as he truly dislikes flip-flops who waiver at the moment of truth," he added as he slammed his glass hard back on the table.

Rodriguez, hands crossed behind his back, legs spread slightly apart, took a small bow, smiled and said in a soft deep tone: "We may also become very good friends Mr. Nobrega. It's all in your hands."

I looked at this trio that seemed zapped right out of a James Bond movie. The corporate manual never mentioned this type of situation, I mused. I had an inner laugh considering this. In fact, I couldn't contain my inner laugh any longer and burst out in a loud hearty laugh.

"Well... well... well," I said in an amused voice, "...*ayayay*... well, I'm glad we considered that possibility." I stretched out my hand, which he shook with an assured smile.

"Alex Nobrega, flip-flop scientist, nice to meet you," I said still laughing. Rodriguez nodded and smiled warmly. His eyes however, revealed a distant coldness, reassuring he would not waiver if push came to shove.

A hard bump shook me out of my pensiveness. I looked at my watch. Still an hour or two to reach Aruba. Colonel Rodriguez was sitting right in front, and looked with somewhat friendly eyes at me.

"Aren't you going to open that folder?" he asked.

"Probably," I replied in a somber tone.

He took something from his breast pocket, a wallet it seemed, opened it up and showed me a picture of two lovely girls.

"Carla and Altagracia, my two daughters," he said with friendly eyes.

"You speak Spanish?"

He looked surprised by that question. "Yeah," he answered. "Why do you ask?" His arm was still stretched showing me the two pictures. I nodded, looked down at the folder in my lap and decided to open it. He placed his wallet back into his breast pocket.

"I'm sorry we had to know each other under these circumstances, but...," he continued.

"Oh God... why me," I interrupted him with a big yawn.

He laughed. "Go on... go on...," he said still in a semi sarcastic tone, "you may need a big friend sooner than you—"

"Shhhht," I interrupted again, this time raising my hand. I stood up and sat next to him, which, judging by his face, took him totally by surprised.

"What do you make of this?" I asked in an urgent voice while showing him one of the pictures.

"Hmmm... looks like... looks like the head of an Egyptian statue, doesn't it? You know, the one with the head of a jackal," he said.

"Exactly! It's Anubis if my memory serves me right. Look at the size of this thing," I whispered. "It looks like some kind of helmet right? Whatever was wearing this must be at least 10 to 15 feet tall I would say."

"What do you think?" he asked in a humorous voice. "Do you think this may be somewhat of a test? Joke maybe? A drill perhaps? I mean this Egyptian helmet looks like a bit prankish don't you think?"

I spread the other photographs. It was difficult to judge anything. The pictures were taken in the wee hours of the morning in a part of the island that is completely dark at night. Flash photography made it all look eerie and spooky, and hard to assess any proportions of it all. It was debris all over, with no reference point like a person standing next to. The only photograph with a man standing next to, pointing to it with a surprised expression, was the one of the Egyptian statue head. I turned the photograph around, and the only strong feeling that kept surfacing about this thing was that it was some sort of helmet or mask. God, this artifact was indeed big.

I looked at Carlos. He shrugged. I shrugged back. I went back to my seat, and started to think again about the whole situation. Why me, I wondered. Why send me, if the organization has the intention to kill whatever crawls out of the debris anyway. Why only the two of us? Who else was into this? Did the Dutch or Aruban government know about our directive? The Dutch should know something, I guessed, as they are the ones finally responsible for international affairs and military interventions. Questions, questions, questions, I pondered.

"Can you ask the pilot to circle around the site before we land?" I asked Carlos. "I want to have a good aerial view of the whole place. It will soon be light when we arrive so we can have a good indication from above of what happened."

He nodded and went to the front. I stretched my legs and started to analyze the whole situation again. Despite the brief differences in opinions and mutual disliking we had in Sauchendaum's office, I had to admit he and the general were right. I cannot ignore what I have read in those horrible books my uncle has in his library about otherworldly creatures that exist all through the universe. Although modern man at the moment cannot prove what others have written millennia ago, if only a small percent was to be true, we might find ourselves in a serious predicament. I shivered as I recalled passages of the notorious *Book of Eibon*. A particular chapter describes rituals required to create, maintain, and close spatial gateways to other dimensions and parts of the universe. A particular frightening description is that of the reign of *Nyarlathotep* and its hordes of servants, beings able to move *not only in the spaces we know, but also between them, un-dimensioned and unseen to us.* Mindboggling paradoxes that had kept me awake for many nights in a row. The doctor and the general were right. There might be creatures out there that we simply cannot take the risk to find out their true intentions...

The plane started to shake vigorously, generating all sorts of squeaky noises. We must be approaching, I thought, as I saw Carlos coming out of the cockpit and gesturing me to come forward to the window where he was standing.

"The pilot will circle a few times around the site," he screamed in my ear. I nodded in approval. Before I knew we broke through the clouds and I saw Aruba in the distance, a brown rusty stain on a deep blue canvas. I always found that sight exhilarating and joyful at first, and yet, as we approach that tiny speck of land in the immense blue ocean, my heart turns heavy in realization that the day will always come I will have to leave again. No matter how many years I have been abroad, in bustling metropolis' or endless country side, the sight of that small rust colored heap of dirt, edged on one side by sugar white beaches contrasting sharply with the turquoise waters, always filled my heart with a strange feeling of sadness and loneliness. There is simply no room for people like me on a small scale community like that, so I'm forced to live as an exile due to its size. Carlos looked at me, as if he sensed my inner struggling. He offered his hand again, which I took this time. There was just no sense in creating extra distractions to an already complicated mission. He pointed to the island in the distance and said "That's us... floating in a vast sea of ignorance about the universe we pertain to. We lie there helplessly, innocently hoping that one day a revelation may wash ashore, not realizing that there are things not meant to be discovered. *Not all doors should be opened just for the sake of opening.*"

"Necronomicon chapter 1," I whispered. He read my lips and nodded. I then and there understood instantly why we have both been chosen for this mission.

The aircraft approached the plain at Alto Vista from the north, flying as slow and low as possible. It then proceeded to circle around the site as tight as possible. The whole northeastern part of the island seemed to be closed off by the local authorities. Cars were parked as far north as the lighthouse and the Alto Vista chapel, with lots of locals standing beside their car trying to catch a glimpse, but further than that there were no one near the crash site, except what seemed a few Dutch marines.

"That's no crash site," yelled Carlos close by my ear. The plane's engines were making conversation almost impossible.

"What do you mean?" I yelled back.

"Look at the way the ground has been moved. Look at the impact mark and how the debris is distributed. Either this craft came exactly 90 degrees perpendicular to the ground, or..."

"...it was an explosion!" I finished his sentence.

The military aircraft finished circling around the site and was heading now west to take a wide left turn to approach Queen Beatrix International Airport. My heart was pounding with anticipation. Little did I knew then that what was to be found would change my life forever...

❈　❈　❈　❈

Forgive me, dear reader, if I skip through the timeline and omit the usual amenities and small details that took place upon arrival. It all doesn't matter to me anymore, as the memories of the past get stronger and instill an overwhelming feeling of unavoidable doom each passing minute while writing this testimony. I often ask myself what's the point, other than relieving my psyche and attaining inner peace. All is lost it seems, and yet, in our darkest hour we must maintain hope. As I stated before, I have remained silent for way too long, and the more 'insiders' I recruit through this document, the stronger we may stand and have a chance when the inevitable hits us by surprise.

We were taken by a military vehicle, as quickly as possible, sirens ablaze, to the site. There, we were welcomed by Lieutenant-Colonel Pieter Boersma from the Dutch Marine Corps. I was somewhat surprised to notice that only a few staff members of the Dutch Marine were there present on site. For such a major event, there were surprisingly few people, maybe five, directly involved on site, none of them from the lower echelons of the marine corps. Many police officials and military personnel were just busy making sure that a huge area, much larger than the actual crash site, was being hermetically sealed to the general public. The enclosed area started from the western most point at the lighthouse all the way to the eastern end of the island, and encompassed the whole northern side of the island including Arikok National Park. All roads leading to this area, from Noord all the way to Sero Colorado, have been closed Lieutenant-Colonel Boersma informed us. He seemed pressed for time. When we arrived at the visible edge of the crash, or whatever happened, Boersma held my arm and in a tense voice said: "We have about nine to ten hours time before the official delegation from Holland arrives. Please do not waste time examining every bolt and nut you find interesting. Focus instead on your mission."

I saw Carlos nodding in agreement. These two are playing in cahoots, I thought, and I couldn't help avoiding the overwhelming impression that I'm being dragged into an operation within an operation within an operation. It reminded me of that strange image you obtain when standing between opposite mirrors; the reflections creating an endless cascade of repeating images ad infinitum.

"What exactly is going on here Colonel, doesn't the Dutch government know we are here?" I just had to ask.

"*That is not dead which can eternal lie....,*" he whispered.

"*...and with strange eons even death can die,*" Carlos finished for him.

Again a quote of that infernal manuscript the *Necronomicon*. The thought of its hideous content send shivers again through my spine; in a strange manner it reminded me of what I suspected to be the real reason for our presence here. *Blessed are those who have not seen and yet have believed[20]*, I thought.

"You made your point Colonel. Come on, we don't have time to waste," I said softly as I opened the manila folder and took the picture of what seemed the head of a giant Egyptian statue. "Can you please take us to this first?"

The whole zone seemed like the set of a post-apocalyptic movie. Destruction everywhere, and the smell of extraterrestrial death penetrated my nostrils. It was an organic smell indeed, but not as we knew it. We stood besides the mask and I was amazed at its huge size. I wanted to take a better look inside, but Boersma warned me just in time.

---

[20] John 20:29

"Don't touch that purplish ooze, it burns like hell. We have one overzealous investigator already in the hospital at the moment."

"What is it?"

"It's organic all right, but nothing as we know of its existence. I would say it's dead alien flesh. Look around, the stuff is everywhere and you must have certainly perceived its smell. The flies seem to want it badly, but even they do not dare to touch it."

He was right. The smell had a repugnant yet sweet odor to it, and everywhere around us flies could be seen frantically circling swatches of this foreign substance; yet not one of them could be noted indulging itself on the matter. I squatted and took a better look inside the head using a small flashlight I borrowed from Carlos. I could see some sort of wiring inside covered by more of the hideous stuff. Flies were buzzing inside the thing without landing on it.

"I think it's definitely a helmet of some sort."

"I agree with you sir, that was our first impression too."

"Look at that. I guess it seemed to be its eyes. The crystalline material is broken due to the force of impact or explosion."

"You also are of the opinion this could have been an explosion?"

"It looks like that, especially when viewed from above."

"How tall do you think the being wearing that helmet could have been?"

"At least more than 20 feet," I replied.

"That's about 7 meters or more right?"

"Yep."

A sharp whistle caught our attention. While we were wondering about the 'helmet', Carlos had wandered off to the east, in the direction of Bushiribana. He waved frantically in our direction, urging us to come as quickly as possible.

"Looks like not all has been killed by the explosion," he said as we arrived. He pointed to the floor. I couldn't see a thing, but the lieutenant-colonel instantly crouched and took a closer look.

"Tracks," he said.

"And it's hurt," Carlos added.

"How do you know, Carlos?" I asked. This was getting a bit too special-ops for me.

"Look back in the direction of the crash site," Carlos said. "Do you see the small groups of flies swirling in the air?"

"Indeed," the lieutenant colonel affirmed. "We must have past them without noticing when we ran up to here to meet you."

I noticed them now. All the way back, at certain intervals of maybe 15 to 20 feet, there were small swatches of flies circling energetically around tiny spots on the ground. It all looked like dots on a piece of paper, waiting to be connected.

"Whatever this is, it got away alive and it's heading in that direction," Carlos pointed to the east, where faintly the ruins of the Bushiribana gold mill could be noticed in the distance.

Lieutenant Colonel Boersma took his radio and gave direct orders in Dutch to his personnel. He emphasized that no one was to cross into the forbidden zone. He then looked at both Carlos and me, and said "Whatever happens from now one, remember this name: Major Karel Apeldoorn. He is my second in command here and the only one who also knows about our mission. He is the only one that can get you out of here in time in case things get complicated."

We started to head east as fast as we could. Carlos proved to be an extraordinary tracker. The patches on the ground with fly infested pockets of air above them were getting less and less frequent, but nevertheless Carlos managed to stay on track. We were pacing ourselves now into a five miles per hour jogging speed, and the rising sun soon made its blistering presence felt. Nevertheless, the adrenaline rush kept us going like hungry cavemen on the hunt. We smelled blood... alien blood!

After about two hours we were way past the Natural Bridge, and well into the ex coconut plantation of Daimari. Colonel Boersma arranged for water to be delivered by a helicopter ordered to follow us from above. Carlos proved to be relentless. We took a short ten minute break at the Natural Pool, or as the locals call it *conchi* or *cura di tortuga*, an open air crystal clear pool enclosed by volcanic rocks sheltering those daring enough to enter the deep pool from the brutal waves of the rugged northern coast. It was here where Carlos seemed to have lost the creature's tracks a bit, but soon enough we heard the familiar sharp whistle again as he found them again. Following the tracks, we continued to move further east towards the most rugged and inaccessible part of Aruba's North coast.

Carlos suddenly stopped. He looked around in the distance further east as if searching for any indication at all of movement. "This creature knows where he's heading," he said in a firm tone. We gazed in the distance where the heat seemed to be boiling the air above the ground.

"How do you know... never mind," I sighed.

"Please hand me your map," Carlos asked the colonel. I looked over their shoulders as both were tracing the north coast on the map with their fingers.

"There!" I suddenly said and pointed to Fontein. It all became clear to me for some reason.

"You know this place?" Carlos asked. "What's there?"

"Of course", the lieutenant colonel expressed enthusiastically. "You may be just right, Nobrega. The caves at Fontein."

"Is there a cave system there?" Carlos asked.

"Yes, and they run very deep underground. Some folks suggest they even extend under the sea all the way to Venezuela."

"Oh Great... can you call that chopper down?" Carlos asked Lieutenant Colonel Boersma.

"Roger that."

We were soon hanging in there in the helicopter heading at neck breaking speed a few meters above ground in the direction of Fontein Cave. Carlos was convinced we would find the creature there. Don't ask me how he did it, but this man seemed to have a dog's nose for these sort of things. Besides, if another military guy such as Lt.-Col. Boersma didn't utter the slightest objection to the handling of Carlos, who was I to doubt the course of action taken.

As soon as we arrived at the cave's entrance, Carlos jumped off and started his 'sniffling' again. This time it was Boersma who found a trace. "Look!" he said, pointing at the corroded metal bars used to close off the cave. A small patch of organic goo was smeared against one of the bars, as if the creature had gripped it somehow to assist himself. The amount of flies circling around it in the air was unmistakable. Flies were also whizzing past our heads into the gaping mouth of the cave. There was no doubt left, we have found it's hiding place.

❊ ❊ ❊ ❊

How long we had been penetrating the insides of the cave I cannot recall at this moment. We were crawling inch by inch, deeper and deeper into all engulfing darkness and madness. Both Boersma and Carlos had their guns out, arms stretched in front of them, eyes bulging with fear and horror at the thought of what may be waiting for us at the end of these nightmarish caves. The air felt thick and pungent with the suffocating smell of bat guano and choking humidity. We were sweating profusely and I could swear I could smell Boersma's underwear.

I felt a hand gripping my arm and slipping a gun into my hand. It was Boersma, who switched guns to a more reassuring Uzi. "Do not hesitate... as we will not," he whispered in my ear. Our flashlight's beams were making a macabre dance against the ceiling and walls. Every square inch was examined before the next step was taken. A thick centipede was trying to hide from my prying beam, and as I followed it to the far end of the chamber, my flashlight's beam hit a slimy glistering figure crouched against the back wall. It made a snarling sound.

Words to describe this creature to convey its hideousness to you my reader, still may elude me to this day, but the necessity for you to have at least the slightest idea of what we encountered that day deep in the caves of Fontein is imperative. This was a monster beyond my wildest imagination. Caught in the three blinding beams of our flashlight it rose from the ground and spread what seemed like arms against the wall behind it. There were four of them. It was about 6 feet high, standing on two massive muscular legs. It's head had about six bulging opaque eyes and had a hideous gaping slit for a mouth showing massive shiny teeth, from which a fleshy thin tongue slid in and out from behind. It shook its head, packed with silicone looking protruding extremities on top, and snarled again at us, the sound of it sending waves of terror through my body, while its arms made slow threatening movements in our direction. We were paralyzed. I looked at Boersma and Carlos standing next to me, and their faces showed that nothing in their secret military training could have ever prepared them for this.

"Spread out ... slowly," Carlos whispered.

"You stand here," Boersma said to me. "Carlos, try to cover as much ground to the right as I remain in the middle."

It became clear to me what Boersma wanted. By covering a wide angle, hopefully we were not all at once in the creature's field of vision, splitting where he could place its attention, if such thing was possible with a being that possessed six eyes. The creature seemed to get the tactical concept also, and became more agitated. It was dressed in what looked like a uniform, or some sort of space suit, which was ragged at the legs and arms by the ordeal it had gone through. At his side, the uniform was ripped and drops of purple grey ooze was slowly dripping to the ground. The sweet pungent stench and the hordes of flies it attracted was overwhelming. The thousands of flies frantically circling the otherworldly beast caused a buzzing background noise reverberating all around the cave. It all made me think of a biblical plague. It was madness straight from an unimaginable nightmare, as the beams of light interrupted by the millions of flies created a surreal stroboscopic effect.

How long we all stood there in this hellish Mexican standoff I have no recollection. The buzzing sound was hypnotizing, as the beast slowly moved its head from left to right... from right to left... endlessly... watching... gauging our strength and intentions. All of a sudden, the beast slowly raised one of its right arms, its four fingered claw opened as if making a gesture of requesting a time out. Its other upper right arms also went open clawed high in the air, while its left inner arm slowly went to what seemed like a breast pocket on its uniform or space suit. The other left arm also went high in the air and shook claws with its upper right arm.

The creature grunted something that sounded like *"Ng graff shibouks..."*

I was going out of my wits, as I had no clue what to do in this maniacal situation. From the corner of my eyes I saw Carlos take a step slowly forward.

"Ng graff shibouks... shibouks," I recall the creature grunting again. Its claw was reaching for something inside its breast pocket. It came slowly out with something rectangular shaped.

"Shibouks...," it grunted again as it slowly opened the rectangular device to show its content. It unfolded in two halves, showing a picture on each side. I couldn't discern them clearly due to the blinding lights reflecting on the shiny surface, but at that moment I could swear they seemed two pictures of similar hideous beings. Carlos took another slow step forwards, aiming his beam of light directly at the open alien device. It seemed indeed two pictures of similar alien beings, although they looked much smaller in size.

Carlos lowered his weapon a bit as he hesitantly said "It... it seems... it seems as if it is trying to show us he has a famil—"

Carlos never knew what had hit him. The alien suddenly, with lightning speed, whipped out a flexible fifth tail-like arm it had kept hidden from behind its back, holding an alien weapon device in its claw with which he instantly fired a fluorescent short laser-like beam exploding Carlos's head clean off. A swift second shot whizzed a fraction of an inch past Boersma's head, which had instinctively let his body drop to the ground as he sounded alarm. A third shot grazed my ear, and to this day I can still feel its infernal heat. The alien never got a chance to fire a fourth shot, as Boersma immediately opened fire from the ground, emptying his Uzi magazine completely on the shaking and trembling alien body, nailing it to the wall. It all happened so damn fast. The next thing I could remember, was the distinct 'click-click-click-click' sound my pistol's hammer made as it repeatedly hit the weapon's empty chamber. I was still in a state of shock when Boersma finally lowered my arm and took the gun out of my hands.

The alien had slipped slowly to the ground by now, making gurgling sounds as the putrid organic ooze slipped extensively out of its body through numerous holes. The colonel reloaded and kept the Uzi aimed at the alien until it gave no sign of life anymore. We then checked the surroundings of its body and found a satchel made of alien material containing various objects unknown to us. As the colonel swayed the satchel on his shoulder, we heard a loud horrible growl deep inside the caves. It was a different sound as the alien at our feet made, but nevertheless felt equally threatening. The sounds didn't progress in our direction, but could be heard retreating deeper into the caves continuing at the far end of the chamber. Something, surely equally horrifying in nature as what lied dead at our feet, was retreating to the deep uncharted depths of the Fontain cave labyrinth. We did not dare to engage its pursue at that time.

Two months had passed since those horrible events took place deep in the Fontein caves in Aruba. News had reached us that in complete secret, Lieutenant–Colonel Boersma and some of his most trusted men had effectively managed the next night to extract the bodies of both the alien and the unfortunate Colonel Carlos Ramirez Rodriguez, may God rest his brave soul. Meanwhile, that same night, a second search party led by Major Apeldoorn successfully located the origin of the horrible growls we heard at Fontein right after killing the first alien. The report send to us showed the picture of a creature dressed in a similar space uniform as the other, with a rubberlike skin and much more humanoid features. It showed two arms and legs, no tail, and a gecko-like face with large eyes. The report stated that this alien showed almost no aggression towards the pursuing unit, which made their 'final solution' type mission much easier. Both alien bodies now reside at a secret place here at the center, where they were dissected and kept for study.

Meanwhile, I kept going at a frantic pace, without the necessary time to have these shocking past experiences processed by my psyche. What kept dr. Sauchendaum and me relentlessly going, was what to make of the strange alien device found in that satchel. I will not bother you with all the complex technical details of our endeavors to figure out what this thing was, but we soon noticed that some of the alien calligraphic symbols covering it had an uncanny resemblance to ancient Egyptian hieroglyphs. When we thought we may had a breakthrough there, none of the writing could be deciphered by hired scientists educated in the ancient Egyptian scriptures. The symbols resembling some ancient hieroglyphs were too few to obtain a sufficient understanding that could have lead to their translation. By the time we were two months further in our investigation, both dr. Sauchenbaum and I were convinced however that this was either a communications, or computer device of some sort.

Great was our exuberant joy when dr. Sauchendaum and I were finally able to crack its power system and make it work. Finally, one late night in January, 1998, we both succeeded in making it produce a humming sound. It showed signs of life! We waited patiently, and all of a sudden the thing projected a 3-D screen on top, filled with strange alien symbols. No sense explaining the painstaking work we did to slowly unravel the inner workings of its operating system, sufficient to say that the horrific content of one of its files took us all, me in particular, completely by surprise.

Again, words may elude me, my dear reader, as how to best describe what we witnessed that cold January night. It all began as the device projected a 'stage' of some sort, a circular area surrounded completely by huge stands, a grand complex similar as the ancient Roman coliseum. The stands were filled with hundreds of alien beings, almost all of them resembling ancient Egyptian statues. They had the same bronze colored humanoid bare-chested bodies as seen on ancient depictions in Egypt, with long muscular arms and legs just as humans, but with all different animal heads, such as Jackals, Bulls, Cats, Hawks and others. They were making incomprehensible sounds and noises, as if speaking in an alien language totally foreign to any syntactic concept to ours. I will resort to familiar concepts like arena, stage, ceremony, show, to attempt to best describe what followed.

A master of ceremonies stepped into the center of the arena. It raised its arms to the ceiling and soon the whole complex went quiet. Needless to say, both the doctor and I couldn't comprehend a single word this giant with the head of a bull was saying, but we both got the impression that some sort of show was about to begin. Sounds similar to music permeated the whole atmosphere.

"Must have one of these stereo sets," Dr. Sauchenbaum joked. I was too fascinated by it all to appreciate any attempt at humor. The floor opened slowly and another being appeared, tall, muscular, fully dressed in fancy robes, wearing a stylized helmet or mask representing a jackal's head, similar as the one we saw at the crash site. The crowd roared as a huge spherical 3D holographic screen descended from above and projected the being with the jackal's mask in such a fashion that everyone in the coliseum must have been able to obtain a clear close up view of what was going on in the arena. The musical sounds went into a crescendo, as the creature produced a giant cage out of nowhere, and started to spin it around its axis as if showing it to be empty. A stunning female figured creature materialized out of thin air, and as the crowd went mad again, it stepped gracefully towards the slow spinning cage. It had the head of a bird, but clearly a chest resembling the bare breasts of a female human. The cage slowed its spinning just enough to let the new creature in, and immediately picked up its rotating motion. The jackal-headed-being threw a giant robe over the spinning cage, which on its turn started to rotate with breath taking speed. It created a magnificent hypnotizing effect as the lights were dimmed all around in the domed coliseum, and the musical sound turned in a sort of drum roll. At the darkest moment in the theater, all sorts of colored light streaks started to emanate from under the cloth's fabric, creating an effect resembling a seventies disco ball. With a loud explosive sound, the jackal-head ripped off the cloth from the gigantic cage, which burst releasing perhaps fifty to eighty odd shaped creatures of all sorts that started to run around frantically in all directions. The crowd went hysterical.

Dr. Sauchendaum jumped to its feet, gripped me by my collar and screamed "MY GOD!... ARE YOU SEEING WHAT I'M SEEING ALEX?"

I stared transfixed at the massive intergalactic pandemonium taking place at the jackal-headed-creature's feet. It was as if a gigantic crate full of monstrous insects had fallen to the ground. All sorts of horrific monsters were running around screaming in terror, some of which I managed to recognize as pertaining to the five-armed or the gecko-type species we killed in the caves at

Fontein. It was then that I realized the gigantic scale of this coliseum type dome, and the enormous size of its spectators inside. None of these hysterical creatures running on the floor at the bottom of the dome reached as high as even the knee of the jackal-headed-monster towering in their amidst. High and above all the ongoing tumult, the jackal-headed-monster roared in a thundering maniacal voice while it spread its massive arms and out of thin air started to produce artifacts such as knives, machetes, axes, spears, spiked clubs and other medieval looking weaponry, which he let fall in massive amounts onto the ground. The frantic creatures rushed as possessed to lay their claws on any weapon they could grab as fast as possible, while the thousands of onlookers in the stand rose to their feet in an ear deafening uproar. Dr. Sauchendaum and I watched in indescribable horror, as we witnessed one by one these beings slaughter each other in the most gruesome manner. The agonizing screams of terror, the clattering of metal against each other, the chopping fleshy sound of steel hacking into bodies, the gobs of strangely colored organic goo flying around, all this carnage, was being expertly filmed by what I guess must have been flying robotic cameras. Their controllers made sure no repulsive detail was left to the imagination.

It was there and then that I saw him, limping, clothes ripped to shreds, his left arm dangling lifeless at his side as if its tendons had been snapped, his blood filled face turned into a horrible grimace with his left eye hanging out of its socket as he faced the close up camera while slashing furiously at an eight legged arachnid looking creature. I slowly rose out of my chair, eyes and mouth wide opened in incredulity, tears flowing down my cheeks as I tried to utter a sound in a voice that was totally gone.

"There!... There!...," I managed to utter in a horrific hoarse whisper. There, amidst an unimaginable pandemonium of galactic proportions, there was my missing uncle, the amazing Doctor Mobuto, the once Master of the Underworld and lord of the Linking Rings; now a mere prop in an intergalactic magic spectacle, fighting desperately for his life. The hunter became the hunted, as if karma indeed knew no borders and spanned the whole universe. A shadow loomed suddenly from behind and with a swooshing sound my uncle's head disappeared from his neck. The last thing I remember watching before I fainted, was his lifeless beheaded body falling into a pool of organic material while a strange crustacean-like creature stepped over it snapping an enormous claw.

❖ ❖ ❖ ❖

3.   Epilogue

Many, dear reader, too many to even start to mention, were the agonizing questions that kept tormenting my mind and soul for many years to come. How did my uncle end up in such a horrible situation? What really happened that fateful day at the Santa Ana mountain? What was his connection to these aliens? Was he helping them? What were these aliens doing in Aruba? Is there a connection between that secret potion my uncle apparently murdered those magicians for and the reason those aliens took him? Was he already for some time in communication with them, or did he just happened to be at the wrong place at the wrong time? Questions and enigmas enough to drive anyone mad, but I leave you my dear reader with this frightening fragment from the infamous *Necronomicon,* that most hideous archive of archaic secrets:

Nor is it to be thought that man is the oldest or the last of earth's masters, or that the common bulk of life and substances walk alone. The Old Ones were, the Old Ones are, and the Old Ones shall be. Not in the spaces we know, but <u>between</u> them! They walk serene and primal, un-dimensioned and to us unseen!

Think about it, let it swirl and seed itself in your psyche. No use in tormenting your mind with the many other horrendous revelations I discovered during countless sleepless nights between ancient and secret pages. Just be aware that mankind may just be insects at the bottom of the universal ecological chain. Be aware that up to now we may only have had just a glimpse of the many otherworldly realities not able to fit into the feeble human psyche. Blessed are those that float in that ocean of darkness and ignorance, unaware and oblivious of many universal truths. Also, be advised and warned that the day may come that unfriendly alien hordes may finally manage to attain a firm and definite foothold at our shores. Recent documents discovered in Jerusalem written by that greatest scientist of all times, Sir Isaac Newton, suggest that this doom's date may be closer than we suspect. The year 2060 is mentioned with great conviction by Sir Newton, a date which he was able to calculate by decoding the cryptic Book of Daniel in the Old Testament[21].

I myself may have little time left. Sixteen years have passed since Dr. Saugendaum and I made those horrific discoveries back

---

[21] These documents written by Sir Isaac Newton were rediscovered in 2007 in an old library in Jerusalem. These, and other secret manuscripts by Sir Newton, are currently at an exhibit at the archives of Hebrew University. They can also be found on the net at the site of Project Gutenberg.

in early 1998. Since then, I managed to attain an early retirement from the agency, and am back at my beloved pearl in the Caribbean. That brave Dutch marine who saved my life at Fontein, Lieutenant-Colonel Boersma, and I have become great friends since then, and many dark nights we set out to camp in the darkest part of Arikok National Park to gaze at the heavens. We watch and observe, we analyze and fantasize about the billions of worlds we now know exist out there. A fact for which we were firsthand witnesses. I hope, through this manifest, I have been able to awaken in you not a mental state of anxiety or despair, but a willingness to confront reality when the times demand your readiness to do so. I leave you now dear reader with one of the most ominous quotes of that infernal and notorious manuscript, known by few insiders as the *Necronomicon*.

That is not dead which can eternal lie,
and with strange eons even death may die...

May you stand firm during future inevitable ordeals.

The End.

Of every tree of the garden thou mayest freely eat: but of the tree of the knowledge of good and evil, thou shalt not eat of it: for in the day that thou eatest thereof thou shalt surely die.

Genesis 2:16–17

Sonata

♪
First Bar: The Package

There exists an interview with every single soul on this planet about music in all its complexity, and each and every soul resonates in accordance with one single fact: Dennis Steenbergen playing his violin is a product from hell, an instrument of torture, the devil's emissary to infuse terror, the creator of the most horrible irreproducible sound in the world; probably, even in the whole universe.

The extended and torturous road of Dennis's maniacal musical creations started that bright August morning when a package arrived at the Steenbergen mansion. Dennis was ecstatic and hyper as if possessed by demons when he finally was allowed to hold and open the package, which was in fact his present for exceptional grades at school and passing to the next grade as number one in his class. It contained the violin he has wished for so long. After unpacking, he placed the violin and bow carefully next to each other on the carpet and lay himself to rest aside, staring in total awe at the beauty of their wooden structure, while occasionally gently caressing both in admiration. His innocent mind was unaware that what he perceived as priceless, had cost a little less than 25 guilders at the local Chinese minimarket. It was the moment he finally picked it up and played his very first few notes, that the thought crossed Maria Steenbergen's mind that maybe, just maybe, it would have been better if she had spent a little bit more on her son's first violin.

❈   ❈   ❈   ❈

Dogs are howling until the deep and darkest hours of the night. Cats are screaming their lungs out. Japanese Koi fish are frantically leaping out of a pond as if in a hysterical attempt to get as far away as possible. Their eyes are bulging as if they were staring at horrific sights, and their mouths are gasping rapidly creating the impression they are actually trying to produce unspeakable cries for help. From an adjacent piece of bush, dozens of boas, centipedes, spiders, scorpions, and other sorts of vermin emerge from dark shadows and frenetically head full speed to the streetlights at the nearby road, where they all cross to the other side engulfed by dark shrubs. Not all make it to the other side though. Cars passing by squish many of them, sending them flying high into the air, creating a bloody fountain of flesh and bodily fluids mixed with eerie strange noises produced at last moments of mortal agony. All this pandemonium is accompanied in the background by faint ominous maniacal sounds produced far away by Dennis practicing his newly acquired violin out of the basement of his house.

❈   ❈   ❈   ❈

♫
Second Bar: The Violin

"Dear all," Maria started, "thank you for coming here and bringing this to my attention in such a nice way. You are indeed the best neighbors one can wish for. I have no words to put this in a logical way, so I will not waste your time with excuses. The sounds you have heard last night came from the violin I gave Dennis as a present."

She instantly raised her hand before anybody could utter a sound.

"Please let me finish," she said firmly. "As I said, I have no logical explanation, but this is the absolute truth. Dennis received a violin yesterday as a present for his extraordinary grades and performance at school, a violin he has wished for since he was a very small boy, and now that he is going to the third grade I decided to buy him one. Maybe not the best decision in my life considering last night's events."

For countless seconds, The neighbors stared at each other somehow bewildered. Then all of a sudden a cacophony of voices broke loose. Maria raised her voice and said "PLEASE! PLEEEAAASE!... One at a time... please... let's not forget why we're here."

"A violin?" Gomez the next door neighbor asked.

"Yes... a violin, albeit a cheap one I may add."

"But how... how... I... I didn't even know a violin could make such a noise."

"Please let me finish explaining," Maria said calmly. "How unbelievable this may sound, it was Dennis who was producing these ghoulish sounds with his violin from the basement until deep into the night. After the first few 'notes' he played, I told him he could only practice in the basement."

"But why didn't you stop him afterwards? Why did you let it go on and on until past midnight? Sorry to say this Maria, but are you deaf? Haven't you heard the awful ruckus all dogs and cats were making? God knows how many souls this violin may have woken up from the cemetery across the street."

Maria let out another sigh. "This may have been all my own fault. I bought Dennis the cheapest violin I could lay my hands on. It came from the Chinese minimarket at the end of the street. By God, I don't know why I did it. I should have bought him a decent one from the music shop down town, he certainly has earned it, but this one, 'made in China', was only 25 guilders and those downtown start at 200. You all know how hard things are nowadays for a single mother. I never expected this! I never thought Dennis would be this obsessed with the damned thing. You should have seen how happy he was when he received it. You all know Dennis. How kind and respectful he is. How was I to break his heart and prohibit him on the very first day he received what he was asking for since he was 2 years old?"

"Hmmm... we all know how special Dennis is all right," Gomez murmured. "I have never seen such a smart kid in my life. Always polite and respectful to you and all of us."

"Yep. The salt of the earth," Anna, Gomez's wife, affirmed.

"May I suggest something in this matter?"

"Oh sure, please do, Franklin, please."

"Yes Franklin, please, be my guest."

"Maria, Gomez, Anna, everyone else here present," Franklin continued, "as his schoolteacher I have to stress on the fact that Dennis is doing extremely well at school; denying him his passions will certainly affect his performance at school, even may have drastic consequences when he starts entering adolescence. So I'll get straight to the point. Why don't we all chip in and help Maria buy a decent violin for Dennis, and maybe even help her out to get him some initial violin lessons at the music school, so he can at least get started in a proper way."

"What? Are you out of your mind? Maria here decides to give her son an expensive instrument, does not have the proper funds, buys the only violin that escaped being fire wood in China, and we have to pay for all this?"

"Anna! Shut up you stupid cow!" Gomez snapped at her.

"No! You shut up!" Anna shouted back.

"No! You shut the fuck up right now!"

"No limp dick, You shut up!"

"I cannot take this any more you fat cow." Gomez said while raising his hand with clear intentions of slapping his wife in the face. Franklin quickly intervened by grabbing Gomez by his wrist. In uncontrollable rage, Gomez turned around and screamed "Mind your own damn business, asshole!"

"Hey! Hey! HEY!" Maria yelled. "This is my house. Show some respect."

"Respect?" Anna screamed above her lungs, "Respect? Do you even know what that means? Look who's talking about respect. Miss perfect here who slept with the prie—"

Maria silenced her with a vicious bitch-slap right across Anna's face. Gomez managed to wrestle his hand out of Franklin's grip and landed a solid punch on Maria's face, which send her stumbling backwards into the large bookcase at the far side of the room. Immediately after that, Gomez felt Franklin's iron grip reaching from behind crushing his testicles, which caused him to succumb with a horrendous moan to the floor. Other neighbors quickly stood up with the intention to intervene and stop this inexplicable madness, but in a bizarre way, all their well intended actions acted like fuel on a blazing bush fire. What should have been a civilized meeting between educated folks, evolved strangely into a vicious brawl which only ended when several police units arrived on the scene and were forced to intervene with even more brutal force.

In the corner of the back yard, perched on its fence, an endemic burrowing owl watched the whole ordeal with hypnotic fascination; his head bobbing up and down as in ecstatic enjoyment, while high above, more and more vultures amassed in a macabre spiraling circle, accelerated by the relentless northeastern trade winds, howling in a ghoulish crescendo as if warning everyone for miles around that something unholy was rapidly approaching.

❖ ❖ ❖ ❖

♪♫
Third Bar: The Cherry

Dennis didn't notice the old man until he was quite close to the foot of the big boulder he was sitting on. The low afternoon sun hid the man's approach from the west through the cacti field, until he seemed to appear out of nowhere next to the big rock. Dennis was startled and stopped playing his violin immediately. As usual, he was embarrassed to practice where anybody can hear him, so he remained still and looked at the old gentleman dressed completely in a white suit, white Panama hat on his head, white cane in his right hand, and a white leash with a white Jack Russell terrier attached to it.

"Well, hello there, son. Go on... please don't let me disturb you from practicing."

Dennis remained silent.

"Do you mind if I join you up there, son, and hear you play for a while?"

Dennis shook his head, and stood up to go help the man climb up the 5 meter high boulder, but when he turned around, the old man was already standing behind him.

"How... how did you do that?" Dennis squeaked in bewilderment.

"Ooh... don't let these white hairs fool you. I keep myself fit you know. I exercise and eat, well, let's say extremely healthy. Besides I know my way around here quite well."

"I have never seen you here before, sir."

"Well, I don't actually live here, you know, but I come here often while traveling in the area and on special occasions, you might say. I do enjoy the tranquility of the _mondi_ (Arubian bush) in the afternoon, just when all the animals are returning from their busy daily chores. But please, please, don't let me disturb you, go on, let me hear something nice."

"I can't play. I am trying very hard though, but everybody tells me it's horrible, so this is the only place I'm allowed to practice so nobody can hear me."

"Hmmm... I see... well just to make sure, can you please play a few notes?"

Dennis started to play the first notes of the common C scale.

"STOP!" the old man said firmly. "I can hear where your trouble lies. Have you had any lessons, son? How long have you been practicing? Please tell me all from the beginning."

"Oh gosh... well... I have to get home soon, and my mom told me never to talk to strangers. It's getting almost 6 o'clock and it's a 15 minute walk to where I live."

The old man smiled, stuck out his hand and said "Antonio Isaias Frigeiro do Nascimento, at your service. And you are?"

"Dennis Steenbergen."

"Well then... now we know each other. I'm an international consultant you might say, a sort of helper, and I have traveled all around the world assisting many people in their needs, so I'm pretty sure I can come up with a solution to your problems, but first of all, Dennis, tell me more about you."

Dennis stared down at his violin in his lap and in a shy soft voice said: "Well sir... I'm now in the 6th grade of primary school... my mom gave me this violin since I went to 3rd grade. I have always wanted a violin, but I am not allowed to play or practice anymore at home... (sigh) everyone tells me I play horrible... at first my teacher and my mom paid for a special music school for me but after a year my tutor told my mom that it's useless and that she is throwing her money away. I have terrible arguments with my mom, I'm sorry... I could never get the tones right and always produced only the most horrible sounds... at least that's what everybody keeps telling me. They took my violin away, and bought me a new one, but it didn't make a difference... So, they brought the violin back to the store and gave me back my old one... (sigh)... things started to go bad at school after they prohibited me to play, so they gave me back my violin on one condition that things get back to normal at school and that I am only to practice here... on these rocks... far away, so no one can hear me."

"Tell me Dennis, do you know how your brain works?"

"The brain? No... uh... is there something wrong with my brain?"

"Well I will keep this simple son... you see... in the brain you have millions of tiny little wires that connect the brain cells with each other... just like the electricity wires at home... and when the lights are out, how do you put them on?"

"You use the switch."

"Exactly! And you, my dear boy, need to rewire some of those tiny switches you have inside your head, and I, my dear friend, have exactly just that for you... Let me see... Ah!... Here they are."

Mr. do Nascimento took out his right hand from his right outer coat pocket, and slowly opened it, revealing three beautiful big round cherries, succulent and lush in color; a deep sinister burgundy with an uncanny resemblance to dark thick blood.

"Oh! Cherries." Dennis cheered. "My favorites. But... how are these to help?"

Frigeiro do Nascimento leaned forward, and while squinting mysteriously, he stared deep into Dennis's eyes.

"Well, well, well dear boy," he whispered, "these aren't ordinary cherries you know. These are magical cherries from a place far away, and they have extraordinary powers son, extraordinary powers indeed."

Dennis shivered as he suddenly became aware of the repulsive strange stench of the old man's breath. Frigeiro noticed this and quickly retreated his face, while at the same time stretching his arm placing the cherries right under Dennis's nose. Their aroma was intoxicating. Dennis had never smelled cherries like these before. As in a trance he slowly reached out, took one of the cherries and placed it against his lips.

"Wait!" the old man yelled. "Before you eat them you must promise me one thing... you will not play a single note on your violin for 7 days... until after exactly this same hour 7 days from today... otherwise the cherries will not work."

"Okay... I will try."

"Trying is not enough son... until next week Thursday at 6:45 in the evening, you are not to touch that violin... otherwise all this has been for nothing and you will never be able to play a decent note ever again. Do you understand?"

"Yes... I... guess..."

"There is one more thing. You eat those cherries and you will become the best, the most famous violin player ever to live, but, as with everything in life son, there may be a price to pay. A terrible unimaginable horrific price in order for you to keep playing well, to keep excelling to unimaginable heights, and one day, one day we'll meet again, and on that day only you will have it in your hands if that will be the day I will have to collect your debt. Now... do you still want to eat those cherries?"

"With price... what exactly do you mean sir?"

"I have told you all you need to know son. It's all right if you have doubts. If you don't feel comfortable, it's no big deal. Just give me back my cherries and I will be on my way. I'm sure elsewhere on this planet there will be another one who wants to be the best violin player ever to live."

Dennis stared trancelike to the cherry in his hand... and then took a bite.

The sun plummeted rapidly downwards, changing its usual orange evening color to a dark burgundy red on its way to the horizon. Dogs started abruptly to howl for miles around the big boulder. Hundreds of black goats appeared running frenetically through the cacti as if scared by an unseen threat. Flocks of parakeets passed overhead screaming their lungs out in an indescribable hysteria, and in the distance, at the edge of the cacti field, thousands of tiny glistering eyes seemed to appear in the shadowy dark bushes.

❖ ❖ ❖ ❖

♬♬
Fourth Bar: The Messenger

"Yeah hello."

"Franklin, good morning, it's me Maria, Dennis has been accepted into the conservatorium! Can you believe that? Who could have thought."

"Wow! Maria that's great news. No it's extraordinary news. When did you hear?"

"Just now. A letter has been delivered from the Amsterdam Conservatorium. I don't know what to say, I can just cry."

"Does Dennis know already? This surely will change his mood. Has everything been okay with Dennis lately Maria?"

"Well... Yes... Sort of... why do you ask?"

"Well... He has been acting not himself in class lately. You know... not like the Dennis we all know. I wanted to ask you this for quite some time now, but it seems to me as if in the last couple of months he has changed a bit, you know. At first, I thought of it as just adolescence, but in the course of time he has developed somewhat of a mean streak, you know... [CLICK]... Hello?... Hello?... Maria are you still there?... Hello?"

There exists an interview with every single soul on this planet about music in all its complexity, and each and every soul resonates in accordance with one single fact: Dennis Steenbergen playing his violin is a product from heaven, proof of the existence of a divine supreme being, God's musical gift to mankind, the creator of the most beautiful irreproducible sound in the world, probably, even in the whole universe.

"Ladies and Gentleman... Mr. Dennis Steenbergen!"

The crowd at The Royal Opera House, London, England, stood up in a deafening thundering roar! The applause was overwhelming, spontaneous, and could be heard for blocks away outside the opera house. Dennis stood there, shining in the middle of a hurricane of admiration, of awe, of respect, of adoration and worship by the crème de la crème of the music world, whom, by the way, paid a hefty price to witness what many considered to be a miracle incarnate. Tears appeared slowly around his eyes like melting ice, merging together to form streams flowing on his cheeks. The world simply has never witnessed a violin virtuoso the likes of Dennis Steenbergen before.

"Damas y Caballeros... El Señor Dennis Steenbergen!"

The crowd at Theatro Colon, Buenos Aires, Argentina, stood up in a deafening thundering roar! The applause was overwhelming, spontaneous, and could be heard for blocks away, outside the theatre building. Dennis stood there, basking in the middle of a hurricane of admiration, of awe, of respect, of adoration and worship. Flowers were thrown at him by dozens of hysterical screaming women, supposedly belonging to the elite of Buenos Aires society, yet, tonight, behaving like enraged teenagers. Dennis took a deep bow, then walked to the stand where he had placed his violin, picked it up, and slowly silenced the audience with the beginning tones of tonight's encore, his now world famous *Sonata di Matadera*. All of a sudden he stopped. A piece of women's lingerie, a lush pink g-string with black lace, fell next to his feet. He picked it up, strung it to his bow, winked at the lady in the front row looking at him in an all too lascivious way, and resumed his master piece. The crowd giggled in awe.

"Gokwái... Steenbergen Sāang!"

Dennis didn't pay attention to the exuberant applause nor the wild cheers of the rich and famous at the Hong Kong Opera house. Although he bowed graciously to receive his standing ovation, and smiled politely to pretend humble gratitude, his mind was racing like a Ferrari on nitro, focusing on one disturbing fact: how the hell did he struck that awful weird note? Did anyone notice it? He looked nervously to the orchestra conductor who was applauding energetically. If anyone would have noticed, it would be him, he thought. Nothing on the conductor's face showed that though. He scanned the wild cheering crowd while smiling shyly. Everything seemed okay... was it his imagination perhaps? It was a fraction of a second, but nevertheless he was damn sure he heard it... a hideous sound not heard since his childhood. He bowed again, raised his violin in the air more confident this time, slightly convinced that perhaps it was all a mind game, maybe the effect of extensive travel or his lately acquired taste for weird party substances. He straightened his back to obtain e better triumphant posture, raised the other hand also high in the air, was about to shout a big "thank you, Hong Kong", when his smile froze on his face and his eyes slit to obtain a better look at *something* that got his attention back in the crowd. At the far end of the enthusiastic audience an elder Chinese man, dressed in a stunning white traditional *hanfu*[22] and classical wide rim hat covering long strands of white hair, was staring straight at him with a faint smile on his lips. Dennis instantly felt a shiver and broke a cold sweat. He took a quick last bow, and disappeared rapidly into the back of the stage with a face as if he had seen a ghost...

---

[22] Classic Chinese clothing.

❖ ❖ ❖ ❖

Dennis woke up when the fat man dressed in a white 3 piece suit sat down next to him on the couch at the VIP lounge of Shanghai Pudong airport. From under his Prada sunglasses, Dennis glared with visible disdain to this 300-pound-plus animal who dared to wake him up from his well deserved crash after a two day crystal meth binge. He shook his head and made an attempt to stand up to look for another couch, when he suddenly felt a hand grab his arm.

"Sorry to wake you up, bud," the man grunted. "Hmmm... let's see... Dennis Steenbergen, case file AUA-040188-75."

Confused and startled Dennis slid back into the couch. "What?... Who are you?... Do we know each other?"

"Oh I'm sorry... forgot your mother always thought you not to talk to strangers. Manuel Joao da Sousa, life insurance, at your service. But you can call me Manny... everybody does."

Dennis ignored to shake the hand offered by the fat man, who began to laugh out loud repeating his previous words. "Life insurance! What a terminology. Life insurance! How can you insure a life? My God, who invents these words... will have a chat with the guys at the marketing department," he continued laughing out loud. "Anyway, never mind," he sighed as he took back his hand. "Let's get back to your case, shall we?"

Dennis made another futile attempt to stand up and move to another couch as far away as possible from this idiot.

"So!" Manuel shouted out loud enough to make him think twice. "You missed a note in Hong Kong, and managed to miss a few more at Taipei, making weirdly horrible yet familiar sounds in the process, hmm? You think a pattern may be developing here?"

Dennis plumped back into the couch. He kept staring silently in front of him, his dark glasses hiding any expression.

"Yep... thought I would get your attention with that."

"What do you want," Dennis hissed.

"Oh not much, bud, not much, just want to make sure you understand the current situation and to insure your life, or salvation, if that term suits you better."

"What situation?"

"Well, let's recap here for a moment shall we? Besides becoming the greatest violinist in human history, amassing a huge amount of fame and fortune in the process, you have also managed to become a selfish, drug addicted, arrogant son of a bitch; with total disregard for other folks' feeling; with a total disdain for human values; using your wealth only to satisfy your egocentric needs." Manny looked at him while tapping on a folder on his knee. "It's all here in your file, bud," he added.

Dennis yawned and stretched his arms. "So? Is there something wrong with that? I am not stealing nor murdering anyone. What the fuck do you care anyway?"

Manny took a long look at him.

"What?" Dennis blurted out. "WHAT? Cat got your tongue?"

Manny took a deep breath. "What happened along the way, buddy? No, you're not stealing, you're not murdering anybody... yet... but you're hurting people in the process of satisfying devious needs, and you're not contributing anything else to humankind except your violin playing."

"Oh Jeez. I think you're not getting the full picture here, mister insurance guy. I'm an extremely well paid clown. People pay me to be entertained, and after that they are just interested in being seen with me for their own interests and status... 'oh look at me standing with the famous Steenbergen at the Krasnapolsky in Amsterdam' ...pffft."

Manny hesitated, and then said, "Not everyone is like that. There are a lot of empty shells indeed, but many others are full of beautiful spirits. Worth the effort and sacrifice."

"Ha! I see you have never been in the lime light before, insurance guy. Ha. What a joke." Dennis sat straight and turned his face to Manny. "Do you really think any of them care what I think, what I feel, what my hopes are for this world? There is so much I would like to do to better this world, but I'm afraid there is no cure for human stupidity. The world is one big hypocritical place, so I'm having a blast until my last string breaks."

"It takes a few seconds of tremor to bring down a building that took ages to built," Manny said with a calm voice nodding his head. "The world is bettered deed by deed. It takes energy to withstand the forces of chaos and create order. You may not see it now, but your actions have great consequences in the overall grand scheme of things. Sometimes all it takes is a small bite from the wrong kind of fruit."

Dennis froze visibly at those words. "What the hell exactly do you mean by that," he whispered.

Manny opened the manila folder on his lap and glanced casually into its contents. "Yeah... I'm afraid it's all here in your file, bud. Let me try to explain this as best as I can, amigo, let me ask you this one question: what is it that makes you proud, what is it in general that makes people proud of themselves?"

"Who cares. Go on, get to the point."

"People take pride in their achievements when these take sacrifice to accomplish. Whatever these achievements may be, it is only when they have exacted sacrifice that one takes pride in it. Sacrifice is the common denominator. You, my friend, were not meant to be a great violinist in the first place. You were born with an honest heart and great intellect, and the right mental attitude to persevere where your passion lies. But things suddenly got too easy. Although it wasn't your fault that your skills grew exponentially to superhuman level, you began to suspect that something wasn't right. And there and then, instead of taking advantage of your acquired power and wealth to uplift your fellow man, you got scared that you would soon lose these one day, and decided to maximize the opportunity to take a lifestyle that you always thought was never within your reach, and in that process, you lost all pride in what you do. You could have done many great things, even while afraid that one day your abilities would vanish. You could have taught others. The essence here, bud, is that you could have contributed so much more to mankind. You received the figurative bag of talents, and instead of sharing with those who have nothing, you made a choice to go the other way; to indulge yourself and spend it all on yourself. You lost pride in many things because they came too easy. You got corrupted by the power you have. You didn't share, it was all you, you, and when in doubt, you again. After a while, you became bored. After all, how many Jaguars or Ferrari's can you enjoy, right? How many top of the line penthouses still make you go 'wow', right? You follow me here, bud? Now, these days, for you to get inspired, you're pushing your moral boundaries. You're experimenting with issues of an increasingly dark nature."

Dennis looked at him with a smirk. "Oh yeah? Like what?"

"Like those underage girls in Bangkok. Damn! Let me lay this out for you as clear as I possibly can buddy: in life there is always a line that should never be crossed. One day you decide to cross that line a little bit. You sample what's on the other side and then quickly go back. The next time, you cross the line again and venture a little further in that new and exciting territory, bearing in mind that you're doing not exactly the right thing, and therefore, you always try to go back as quickly as possible. However, little by little you risk penetrating deeper into uncharted regions until you realize that you can't go back. You have exceeded the boundaries of your inner map and lost your way. Understandably, you became ashamed of that because you thought that would never happen, but unfortunately, your inflated ego prevents you from asking for help, and so you push yourself further into a dark abyss, fooling yourself that you have control and that sooner or later you will get out of the woods. Meanwhile, you're acquiring a dark taste for things with an unspeakable morbid and perverted nature; which at the end makes it even harder to ask for help and beg for forgiveness. It's not entirely your fault, bud. You had an enormous potential for good in you. You *still* have, but you were sidetracked... *They* got to you before *we* did. Unfortunately, it's a war out there, bud, and *They* have the upper hand. You see, it's easier to break and corrupt things than to build and maintain them. Shit happens, good souls go astray, but it's never too late to get back on the right path. Let me help you, bud, please allow me to help you. However, I must warn you that I *cannot* force you to do anything, it must happen of your own free choice. Allow me to explain our insurance policy, and maybe we can work things out..."

❖ ❖ ❖ ❖

"...*work things out*..."
"...*it's never too late*..."
"...*work things out*..."
"...*there is still a chance*..."
"...*insurance policy... second chance... together... work things out... it's never too... ring... ring... ring... ring... ring*..."

The phone at the penthouse suite at The Tokyo Imperial Hotel, rang incessantly. Dennis stood up with the biggest hangover imaginable and finally answered the cursed thing.

"Hello," his voice cracked.

"Where the fuck have you been?"

"What?... Who is this..."

"It's Mathew, you moron. Where the fuck have you been? Why didn't you show up in Singapore? What's this I hear you being escorted to the airport by the Singapore authorities and kicked out of the country. What's all these stories about whores and lewd parties I've been hearing about lately. Why the hell do I have to pay a private investigator to find out where you are dammit. Why don't you answer your phone? You have your poor mother worried sick, and she and that school teacher friend of hers are driving me mad with questions I can't answer. What the fuck happened in Hong Kong? You have any idea what that hotel suite you tore apart will cost us?"

Dennis started to cough. "Uh," he spat out, "you have any idea what time it is over here? It's 4 o'clock in the morning, can't we discuss this at noon when I wake up?"

"I'm your agent, Goddammit! I can call you whenever I want for fuck's sake, especially if you're turning yourself into a candy nobody wants to eat... [CLICK]... hello? HELLOO? ...Dennis you fucking piece of shit... don't you dare... Damn!"

❧ ❧ ❧ ❧

A soft knock on the door could be heard through the heavy metal music inside the presidential suite at the President Roosevelt Hotel, Geneva, Switzerland. Dennis stumbled stoned as a mule to the door and swung it open.

"Mom!" he yelled with a heavy tongue. "Well, what a pleasant surprise. All alone? Not accompanied this time by that queer schoolteacher? Come on in. Meet the girls." Dennis grabbed Maria's arm firmly and violently pulled her inside the suite, slamming the door behind him. Maria stumbled against a sofa and fell eagle spread on the floor. A few scantily dressed girls sprung from the sofa, tumbling the small table in front of it, spilling all the neat lines of cocaine onto Maria's face and into her hair. Maria sneezed. She felt her arm being yanked again and she forcibly had to stand up.

"Come on... don't be shy... here you have Miko from Japan and Hai Ping from Hong Kong."

The bathroom door opened and two naked girls, visibly under age, sprung out to see what all the sudden ruckus was all about. Maria tried to say something but the syllables were slapped violently out of her mouth by Dennis. Before she could try to utter another sound, Dennis grabbed her firmly with his right hand around her mouth, his left hand yanked her head back by her hair, while his bloodshot red eyes tried to focus on her face, which was contorted by incomprehensible fear. Amidst frantic guitar riffs of *State Prison*, Aruba's famous heavy metal band, the girls were running around the room trying to find any decent piece of garment to put on before getting the hell out of there.

"Roar lion, roar! You're the king! The jungle is yours! Roar lion, roar! Let them know the king is here..." *State Prison* was making their statement loud and clear from the Bose surround system.

"EVERYBODY STAY AS YOU ARE!" Dennis screamed on top of his lungs. "What the fuck am I paying you for. Our guest of honor," he smirked, "is leaving in a few minutes anyway." He turned angrily towards Maria's face. She could not only smell, she could feel the alcohol and drugs in Dennis's breath hit her face as an invisible wall. She uttered muffled sounds, her eyes bulging in total disbelief.

"What did I tell you about paying me surprise visits, mommy dear, hmmm? WHAT DID I TELL YOU?" He swung the door open, and dragged her into the hallway. "GOODBYE MOM." he screamed sadistically, as he pushed her away.

Maria stumbled violently through the long hallway, propelled by the strength of Dennis's push. Finally, she fell to a halt at the shadowy end of the long corridor, in front of the feet of an old man dressed in a white suit, white Panama hat on his head, white cane in his right hand, and a white leash with a white Jack Russell terrier attached to it. *State Prison's* famous *Post Mortem* started to resonate loud through the hallway... *"Hear oh hear... have no fear... the witches are near and black mass is about to start"*

Dennis's eyes bulged in horror. He turned around in panic and started to run towards the other end of the hallway. The door frames swooshed by his face as it contorted in indescribable fear. He looked back, eyes bulging more in immeasurable despair when he realized the distance between him and his nemesis remained the same. He squinted his eyes, trying to focus at the unbelievable sight he was perceiving. Was the old man floating towards him? His legs didn't seem to move, yet he was catching up. How was this possible? Still looking back in disbelief, Dennis smacked hard against the huge glass window at the end of the corridor. A soft, muffled, cracking sound could be heard as the window shattered in a thousand fragments. Dennis stared in shock at the old white man who was now standing just a few meters behind him in his impeccable white suit, his white Panama hat slightly tilted to the side, the white Jack Russell terrier sitting next to him, staring back with a faint red glow in its eyes. Dennis's incredulity turned into harsh realization as he turned his head back and looked in horror at the deep abyss in front of him. *This isn't supposed to be here next to a five star hotel*, he thought. Gravity started to do its job and Dennis fell into the dark ominous deep with a faint reddish glow at the unfathomable bottom. His scream was soundless as he turned and looked up to the thousands of stars banded together in the milky way, getting smaller and fading while he fell into the deep. In the background, *State Prison's* lyrics faded away...

"*Rejoice, the Yellow King is here.*
Rejoice, for his evil reign is near...
Hail!
Hail!
Hail, oh Hail The Yellow King!
A thousand years of pain is here!
Hail, oh Hail The Yellow King!
Morituri te Salutant![23]
Hail, oh Hail The Yellow King!
Mors vincit Omnia![24]
Hail!
Hail!
Hail, oh Hail The Yellow King!
Macte Animo![25]
This is the road to a thousand years of pain!"

❖ ❖ ❖ ❖

---

[23] Those about to die salute you!
[24] Death conquers all!
[25] Young, cheer up!

Fifth Bar: Coda

Antonio "Tony" Curiel woke up drenched in sweat, screaming his lungs out in unspeakable horror; his wife shrieking alongside him, startled into wild hysteria by his maniacal, long, loud outcries of terror. In the corner table of their bedroom, the alarm clock was making its usual morning ruckus: the tunes of Antonio's favorite *State Prison* song, *Hail The Yellow King*. The air was impregnated with fear, as a long silence settled in with only their heavy breathing as background echo.

"What the fuck was that?" Angelina, his wife asked with eyes wide.

"My God... my God... *coño*[26]! What a horrible dream... my God..." Tony whispered. Angelina took the corner of the bed sheet and slowly started to wipe his face.

"*Coño*... what a nightmare... whew!"

"Don't tell me," Angelina murmured. "You have been dreaming about violins again."

"Hmm hmm."

"Oh my God honey, when will this end?"

"I have no idea dear," he sighed. "It has been quite some time, a year maybe after the last episode?"

"Yes but I have never seen you like this before. You were screaming in an incredible frightening way."

"I realize that now, dear, but this time it was different, totally different."

---

[26] Classic Papiamento curse, used for multiple purposes. E.g. This is a *coño* situation.

Tony got out of bed and started pacing in the room.

"I dreamed about this small kid named Dennis Steen... Steen-something who got this cheap violin as a present. That kid wasn't me and yet felt somehow recognizable. I mean nobody in that dream was familiar, and still that unknown boy felt like it was me. Do you remember the big boulders at Matadera, about 15 minutes into the *mondi* at the back of my parents house in Aruba?"

"Yes."

"Well that's the only place in my dream that was really familiar. That, and the arguments at home with the kid's mother. The kid played the violin in a horrible way, creating diabolical sounds not found in any scale, and thus, was banned by the whole neighborhood to practice in the middle of the *mondi* on top of those boulders at Matadera. I can only remember flurries of it, but this dream was definitely awkward and different to all others..."

Tony continued telling Angelina details of what he remembered: the agony of the kid not able to produce a single decent tone on the violin; the arguments the kid had with his whole family because he wanted to be a violinist, while his mother wanted him to become an accountant, just like his deceased father. He also told her about the white man in the suit, the cherries, the turnaround in the kid's playing skills; the rise into fame and glory; the downfall due to the inability to handle power and fame; the horrible hallucinations induced by unknown drugs; the atrocious mean way the kid turned out to be as an adult; the horrendous confrontation at the end with the kid's mother and the abominable way he treated her; finally, the sudden ordeal with the old man in white.

Tony went into the living room and stood in front of the large glass cabinet containing his violin collection, from his first cheap violin while at primary school, to the Stradivarius he recently bought here at an auction in Amsterdam. Angelina came next to him and lay an arm around his shoulder.

"I'm sorry you have to go through this again dear," she whispered. "I know how much since childhood you have always wished to be an orchestra violin virtuoso, but honey, we have to live with the truth, as Dr. Hanenberg said... only a very few achieve that level of virtuosity. You play at a more than decent level, but no more than that. It's not in you... besides, you are much better at accounting, otherwise you would have never made partner at the firm at the age of 29." She finished giving him a small peck on the cheek. She then grasped his head with both hands and swung his face towards their huge living room window looking out on a spectacular early morning sunrise over Herengracht, Amsterdam. "It's nearly 7 o'clock, you must start preparing to go to work. Big presentation today, remember? BMW board of directors... ring a bell, my Paganini? Or shall I say, Pagan-nini?"

Tony smiled. "You're right love... as usual, and yes I love my job as an accountant, no regrets there. Some things are just not meant to be. Okay, come on, off I go into the showers and you are joining me there for some quick, impromptu, private stress therapy."

Although the head office of Jansen, Laurent, & Curiel was in walking distance from his 17th century house at the famous Herengracht in Amsterdam, Antonio realized he would never make it in time this morning. The block he usually walked through, was completely closed off by local police and national royal guard. Something to do with a possible terrorist attack, code red. He quickly called his secretary and informed her of the situation, asking her to make arrangements to deal with the sudden emergency. He looked at an app on his smartphone and quickly established the shortest walking route towards his office.

The alternative route took him through a part of town riddled with alleys he has never been to. Small shops, dealing in all sorts of curiosa, adorned both sides of every picturesque alley he went through. He often caught himself standing in front of the shopping windows admiring things he never knew even existed. He called his secretary again explaining that his journey towards the office may take a little longer.

When he finished his conversation, he remained paralyzed, staring at a small window. His eyes had caught sight of the most beautiful violin ever imaginable. A stunning piece of craftsmanship. He stood there breathless, in complete awe. He got closer to the window to obtain a better look, and his arm stretched to the window's glass surface, touching, as if caressing this incredible work of art, totally mesmerized by it. He leaned forward placing his face against the glass, and in the back he saw an elderly gentleman leaning behind a counter, gazing downwards, probably reading something. He stepped back a few steps and looked at the sign above the door: "da Conceição & Melo-Silva, violins and musical antiques", it read.

The bell attached to the door made a soft tingling as Antonio opened it. The atmosphere inside the ancient store was damp and stuffy with the smell of antiquity and old books, which were aligned in numerous shelves against all four walls. The elder gentleman looked up, took his reading glasses off, and with a soft friendly voice asked "Good morning, *meu querido*[27] *amigo*, how can I be of service to you?"

---

[27] my dear beloved, in Portuguese.

"I... I... uh... I was admiring your violin in your store's display. Is it possible I could take a closer look at it please?"

"Ahhh... *o Fraqueza do Paganini*[28]? Well sure *senhor*. Please allow me to get the keys to the display. *Por deus, senhor*[29], you have an exceptional eye for quality. Not many recognize this hidden treasure."

The old man opened a drawer next to him, and glimpsed at its contents while a faint anxious smile appeared at his lips. Inside were a pair of white gloves, a set of keys, and in a small white marble bowl lay three gorgeous big round cherries, succulent and lush in color; a deep sinister burgundy with an uncanny resemblance to dark thick blood...

♫♫♫♫   THE END   ♫♫♫♫

---

[28] Paganini's weakness. *Fraqueza* means a.o. weakness.
[29] By God, sir, in Portuguese.

"Don't make the mistake of thinking that the cosmos gives a damn one way or the other about the especial wants and ultimate welfare of mosquitoes, rats, lice, dogs, men, horses, pterodactyls, trees, fungi, dodos, or other forms of biological energy."

Howard Philip Lovecraft
American writer (1890 – 1937)

The Rift

They came at night. Silently, in total stealth, inspiring an ominous feeling of unspeakable doom, they pierced the darkness of his bedroom, and stood around his bed in a conspiring fashion. A sinister ritual that has repeated itself beyond his knowledge for the last couple of nights. That night was the same as the previous ones, where they stood there for what seemed an eternity, whispering to each other in incomprehensible archaic sounds while they seemed to admire and cherish their prey; the innocent body of an unsuspecting man sound asleep, unaware of the terrible peril that had just penetrated the intimacy of his room. Occasionally they would bow closer to his unwary body, sniffling obsessively with joy as if absorbing the taste of his essence, and through the darkness surrounding his bed, brief flashes of glistening eyes could be observed, foul sinister teeth would show themselves grinning in short threatening moments, and the faint murmur of their conversation would rise and fade while they discussed their sinister intentions.

It was not the abominable foul stench penetrating every crevice of the room, nor the faint glow of their pale rippled hands which sometimes protruded briefly from beneath their ancient robes, nor even the incessant hissing of their demonic dialog that awoke Randolph Erasmus from his sleep. It was but a single ice cold glob of drool that suddenly fell from one of the grinning jaws, right onto his cheek. He suddenly opened his eyes wide and felt an enormous gripping fear clench his body. Totally paralyzed, but in complete consciousness, he laid there in impotence while he felt the glob of drool slowly slide down his cheek, resting finally at the corner of his mouth, filling him with an atrocious taste unknown to human souls. A slight cold draft could be felt as the beings seemingly enjoyed his horror, as they slowly began to glide back into the ever absorbing darkness. Still unable to move a single fiber in his body, he saw them disappear one by one, dissolving into the total obscure numbness surrounding his bed. Finally the last one had withdrawn, its glistening sinister eyes fixed upon his paralyzed body, hissing what seemed an obscure prophecy. It was then, after what seemed hours of unparalleled maniacal fear, that Randolph finally was able to utter the most horrendous scream ever to escape a human throat. A scream that was heard for miles around, and which awoke half of the sleeping population of Oranjestad, capital city of Aruba.

Neighbors found him lying there completely unconscious, though with incessant heavy breathing, as if witnessing indescribable horrors through macabre archaic dreams. Paramedics wondered at the incredible stiffness of his body while they carried him to the ambulance, and for the next 48 hours medical personnel of Horacio Oduber Hospital at Bushiri were kept puzzled by the mysterious spastic waves that would ravish his entire body. Finally, after two exhausting days, he woke up wondering in total bewilderment about his strange whereabouts. It took another five days for him to slowly regain his ability to speak and his sense of balance. His days were then spent by wandering the large corridors of the building, gazing in total apathy to what seemed an imaginary horizon. Finally after two weeks, medical personnel felt confident that he was able to be on his own and that he was ready to be released. It was on a bright Thursday morning on October the 31st that the medical staff brought him the news he had feared most for the last couple of days: he would be released to return to his home.

In complete silence he accepted his faith and remained still for the rest of the day as he watched the bright tropical sun slowly descend to the west. He cherished every manifest of pure life as birds sang in the trees as the island's trade winds played their symphony. Finally the moment came when he had to leave, and throughout the ride in the cab he would secretly sob as he gradually approached his neighborhood. At the end he remained in complete solitude standing in front of his house down in Fahrenheitstraat, as he observed what was the window of his bedroom. The same room he knew he would have to spend yet another night facing the ominous fact that somewhere in there ... somewhere in the shadowy borders between modern day reality and archaic surrealism ... *they* were patiently waiting.

❧ ❧ ❧ ❧

For countless moments Randolph stood silently in the middle of his bedroom, contemplating somewhat with a deep distrust the undisturbed appearance of the environment. To the uninformed, the room looked as if it had never been violated by unexplainable phenomena, as if never fouled by such an abominable stench better left un-described to human psyche; au contraire, it created even the illusion that the most horrendous experience of his life was just another nightmare to be ignored. His bed looked untouched, the small collegiate desk organized and tidy, the bookshelf without a trace of dust, and even the magazine he used to read himself to sleep that fatal night laid innocently on his bed. He inhaled deeply, as if trying to detect the most minimal disturbance in the lavender aroma left by the cheap disinfectant used to clean the room. He finally exhaled slowly, hoping by now to exhume the suffocating anxiety he had felt since leaving the hospital.

A sudden and sharp knocking on the front door brought him with lightning speed back to a full state of complete alertness. He held his breath for what seemed endless minutes, and there it was again, maniacal knocking, vibrating this time with what seemed a dark tone of urgency. He summoned himself to start moving slowly towards the front door, feeling an indescribable sense of approaching doom through his exhausted and ravished mind. The knocking started again, anxious and with a crescendo revealing a hidden agony. As he approached the door in complete silence and feeling a suffocating sense of anguish, the by then maniacal and incessant knocking stopped abruptly as if his proximity at the front door has been detected in some unexplainable way at the other side. The sudden and almost deafening silence that followed was softly interrupted by a soft female voice behind the door ...

"It's ok professor... *he* is here."

Randolph, completely surprised by what he just heard, opened his mouth and felt only empty air leaving his throat as he was unable to utter any sound. The overpowering silence that followed was suddenly interrupted this time by an uncompromising male voice.

"Mister Erasmus, with the utmost notion of urgency I beg you, please open the door. We mean you no harm but it is crucial we have a word with you".

Where he extracted the courage from he did not know, but slowly composing himself he managed to cautiously open the door. There on the footsteps stood an odd looking middle aged man, dressed in an impeccable white shirt with a colorful bow tie and covered in a wrinkled old fashioned coat. A man totally unfamiliar to him and yet inspiring him with a strange sense of trust by the open and fearless way the man looked into his eyes. On the man's left hand side was a pale and innocent looking young lady, staring at him with surprisingly sad round eyes, revealing a much greater knowledge and understanding of life and its mysterious ways than one would guess by the simple and juvenile ways of her looks. On the man's right hand side stood a small boy, dark pitch black hair and eyes, sweating heavily on his forehead while holding the man's hand firmly and shifting his eyes incessantly everywhere, as if attempting to absorb as many details as possible. To Randolph the most disturbing of them all however, was what seemed an extremely old individual standing in the back, his position shifted in such a way as to reveal as little as possible of his features. Randolph restlessly tried in vain to obtain a better glimpse, but in an unexplainable way the sinister character was able to anticipate each and every attempt. The only distinct feature Randolph was able to observe was what seemed an ancient suitcase the man carried in his hand, and the black wide brimmed hat concealing what he perceived briefly as a gray featureless expression.

Once again the man in front spoke, this time softer, though expressing the same anxious urgency.

"Please Mr. Erasmus, we do not have much time left. May we come in?".

Randolph, feeling a strange premonition of upcoming dread, softly complied with the man's petition. He stood there silently besides the door, accepting what seemed an incomprehensible sinister faith, while he observed how the dread inspiring group entered one by one into the living room. Again, entering as last, the disturbing and featureless character displayed an amazing ability to anticipate each and every inquisitive attempt made by Randolph to gaze at his facial appearance.

The group sat randomly on the available couches, except for the young boy who kept wandering nervously around and the silent dark character who instinctively chose the antique chair in the corner, which received the less light of all. Each and everyone remained silent for a brief moment while they were arranging themselves in the room. At last the middle aged man, by now perceived by Randolph as being their leader, broke the ever present silence.

"Allow me to briefly introduce ourselves Mr. Erasmus", he said in a soft but firm voice, "My name is Prof. Arturo Leyba, and I'm the head of the faculty for paranormal studies at the Miskatonic University of Arkham, Massachusetts. The young lady sitting next to me is my personal assistant, Miss Ashley Moore, one of the most gifted psychics ever to exist and already by her young age in possession of a PhD in psychiatry. The young boy you see wandering restlessly around, Mr. Erasmus, is known to us only by the generic name of Timmy. He is autistic, with a rare gift which I will explain later, and which will prove to be invaluable for our purposes here."

Randolph nodded silently and gazed with a curious expression in the direction of the dark featureless figure sitting in the shadowy corner. Prof. Leyba cleared his throat nervously and continued.

"Oh yes ... Hum... Eh... Mr. Figeiro of course. Eh...   If you don't mind Mr. Erasmus, I rather not introduce him at this moment but preferably in a later stage, when ... how shall I put it ... your level of comprehension of the whole situation is in a manner of speaking, say, eh ... more advanced?".

Leyba quickly looked into the corner, and then leaned conspicuously in Randolph's direction, staring firmly into his eyes while whispering in a soft but firm manner:

"Rest assured however Mr. Erasmus that your present sanity is for a great deal the result of this man's restless efforts and great understanding of matters better left unexplained to mankind."

Randolph was visibly shaken. His hands started to tremble incessantly while attempting to wipe his forehead. Prof. Leyba leaned back and suddenly, totally unexpected, gripped the wandering boy quickly by the arm, pulled him up in front of his chair, and stared him firmly in the face, while whispering anxiously:

"Are we safe? Are we safe Timmy?".

In horror Erasmus observed the sudden expression transforming the boys face in a grotesque mask, his eyes rolling to the back of his small head; his lips grinning revealing horrendous teeth; his complexion rippling in a manner incomprehensible to any sane human mind.

"Yes Professor... *They* are not here... *Yet!*".

Randolph covered his mouth in maniacal fear. That voice. That horrendous vibration no human ear should ever hear. He knew that voice! In a fluent terrifying cadence brief flashes of horrendous nightmares went through his mind, of sights and sounds bewildering to any human senses, of screams erupting from vast dark voids, of excruciating pain cutting to the bone and impossible to be comprehended by the human psyche, of evil expressing the most unholy desires ever to have reached a human soul!

"The dreams," Randolph whispered as he slowly stood up staring Prof. Leyba in total bewilderment, "The dreams ... Oh my God, the dreams!"

"Yes, the dreams," said the dark figure in the corner as he spoke in a deep ominous voice for the first time while rising slowly from his chair and moving imperceptibly in the direction of Randolph Erasmus.

"Ooohhh, yes, the dreams," he said. "If man only had knowledge of the terrible and atrocious abysses awaiting him while asleep he would never ever close his eyes so confidently. And yet, every night, with the most foolish audacity, man quietly goes to bed ... exposing his mind to unspeakable risks."

Randolph could not but utter a loud shriek as he contemplated the man's face for the first time. That face. That horrendous ash-gray expression marked deeply by years of experiencing maniacal fears and witnessing sights not meant ever to be contemplated by the human mind. That stone cold face. He has seen it. He has felt this man's presence during those first nights of unmentionable terror at the hospital. He has felt his mysterious gaze during those long walks in the corridors.

The man slowly put his arms on Randolph's shoulders and softly whispered.

"Please sit down Mr. Erasmus. What has puzzled you all these days has been my torment and reality for decades. I've worked much too hard to regain your sanity, please don't let it all be in vain. Please, what is to come tonight requires all your strength. Let Prof. Leyba explain it all."

Randolph Erasmus sat down staring at the man's gothic face. Ms. Moore aided him with a glass of water, while Prof. Leyba leaned over and looked at him with those trust inspiring eyes.

"Mr. Erasmus, what I'm about to tell you, better said, what I'm about to reveal, may seem to you   as totally ludicrous, yet it is simply the naked truth."

Erasmus stared in front of him, clenching to whatever remained of his frail sanity.

"Yes. Go on," he whispered.

"Mr. Erasmus, you have had an extraordinary experience, something no one ever wishes to be part of. Yet you had no choice, as you have been targeted by *them* as *their* conduit. We are here to prevent that from happening."

Erasmus looked at him with tears in his eyes. Suddenly he snapped.

"Can you please speak English? Excuse me for having dropped out of Mumbo Jumbo University!"

Leyba softly put a hand on Erasmus's arm.

"I'm sorry Mr. Erasmus, allow me to use what little time we have left to enlighten you with a terrible secret. Have you ever heard of what is commonly known as *demonic possession?*"

Erasmus nodded silently.

"Well Mr. Erasmus," Leyba continued, "that phenomenon that has been perceived through the ages by every single culture on this planet, however remote, is something far beyond any human comprehension. Since the dawn of mankind, people have whispered in hidden conglomerations about forces beyond their understanding. As humanity evolved into more advanced civilizations, names were given to this. Some call it evil spirits, others call it demons; religious authorities call it the devil, or Satan if you like. However only a very few know exactly the true horrendous nature of what is really going on. Only a few of us know the truth about *the ancient ones* ... only a very few are aware of the existence of *Yog-Sothoth.*"

Randolph couldn't help but close his eyes and moan in soul wrenching pain. That name! The secret chants he heard incessantly during his first nightmare. The immense thundering roar of *Yog-Sothoth*! He slowly opened his eyes and nodded.

Leyba leaned further in Randolph's direction, eyes wide open, asking anxiously:

"You have heard of this name?".

"Yes," Erasmus whispered.

Leyba turned to Figeiro and said: "My God, *they* have regained more power than we have expected! We must act swiftly tonight ... before the *unholy hour*!".

He then turned back to Randolph.

"Mr. Erasmus, again I must emphasize that what I'm about to tell you will sound totally incredible, even absurd if you like, but you must believe me that it is nothing more than the truth and that the well being of humanity may well depend on the outcome of the sinister events about to take place here tonight, right here in your very home. Even as we speak, dark events with origins going back to before the dawn of human existence are taking place which may change reality as we know it."

Leyba went to the strange and ancient looking suitcase and opened it. From there he took a thick and extremely old book, bearing strange archaic marks on its back. He held it in front of him gazing it with respect, one might even say fear. Everyone in the room, except Randolph, who was still in the dark what this was all about, stared with the same awe, an indescribable mixture of fear and respect, to the mysterious archaic book. In a solemn tone of voice Leyba continued.

"This here that you are privileged to behold Mr. Erasmus is the notorious, one may even state infamous, manifest of darkness written by the Arab philosopher Abdul Alhazred in the 7th century A.D.; the much dreaded and sought after, *Necronomicon*[30]."

Prof. Leyba placed the book with a slow respectful gesture on the table in front of Randolph, who contemplated its elaborate and sinister symbols on the front, which in a strange way instantly inspired him with visions of dreadful archaic secrets.

"I have no clue whatsoever what this is, or what all this is all about," Randolph said eyes glued to the strange book, "but somehow it smells, sounds, looks so familiar. It's like I have seen all this before. In my dreams perhaps ... I'm not sure, but something tells me I was once part of all this."

Leyba looked at Figeiro, who's face went ash white. Figeiro pouted his lips in the direction of Randolph who was now kneeled in front of the table, eyes mesmerized on the unholy book and slowly caressing it. "*Look* ..." Figeiro whispered.

Prof. Arturo Leyba, a man who has committed his whole life discovering the most darkest paranormal secrets of our

---

[30] **Necronomicon**. A.K.A. *"The book of dead names"*. Original title *Al Azif -- azif* being the word used by Arabs to designate that nocturnal sound (made by insects) supposed to be the howling of daemons. Composed by *Abdul Alhazred (Abd al-Azrad. Abd = servant; azrad < zarada = to strangle or devour; thus, "servant of the great strangler or devourer")*, a mad poet of Sanaá, in Yemen, who is said to have flourished during the period of the *Ommiade Caliphs*, circa 700 A.D. He visited the ruins of Babylon and the subterranean secrets of Memphis and spent ten years alone in the great southern desert of Arabia -- the *Roba el Khaliyeh* or "Empty Space" of the ancients -- and "Dahna" or "Crimson" desert of the modern Arabs, which is held to be inhabited by protective evil spirits and monsters of death. Of this desert many strange and unbelievable marvels are told by those who pretend to have penetrated it. He claimed to have seen fabulous *Irem*, or City of Pillars, and to have found beneath the ruins of a certain nameless desert town the shocking annals and secrets of a race older than mankind. In his last years Alhazred dwelt in Damascus, where the *Necronomicon (Al Azif)* was written, and of his final death or disappearance (738 A.D.) many terrible and conflicting things are told. He is said by Ebn Khallikan (12th cent. biographer) to have been seized by an invisible monster in broad daylight and devoured horribly before a large number of fright-frozen witnesses. Testimonies left by his peers illustrate that his uncontrolled and ravaging madness was the result of fanatically worshipping unknown entities whom he called *Yog-Sothoth* and *Cthulhu*.

---

universe, a man who has seen things unimaginable by uninitiated minds, a man not easily scared or disturbed, stood up slowly, eyes fixated on what, to inexperienced onlookers, would look like a feeble broken man caressing an old book with trembling hands while whispering inaudible sounds to it. He felt a small hand gently grab his left hand. It was Timmy.

"Professor," Timmy whispered as not to disturb the trance like state Randolph was in. "*They* are close, doctor, *they* are very close ..."

A sudden loud knock on the door made everybody jump in unison. Ms. Moore let out a loud shriek, while Timmy screamed his lungs out. Figeiro instantly whipped an ancient relic from his coat's inner pocket and pressed his lips against it while whispering ancient prayers. Randolph bolted backwards with a loud gut wrenching growl while his eyes rolled to the back of his head as if he was fighting whatever was trying to keep him in his trance like state. Doctor Leyba lunged forward and slapped Randolph hard several times in the face. Slowly Randolph's gaze returned to normal. His expression however, indicated that he probably wasn't aware what had transpired the last couple of minutes.

Another louder knock on the door. "Open up! It's the police!" a deep voice yelled outside.

Ms. Moore opened the door and said "Inspector Rasmijn, special agent Tromp, welcome, how can I be of assistance?"

Inspector Frederik 'Freddy' Rasmijn stood there frozen, completely caught by surprise by Ms. Moore's assertion of their names. '*How the hell was this possible? What's going on here?*' raced through his mind. He barely was able to mumble a few words when Prof. Leyba stepped aside Ms. Moore and gently invited him in. Inspector Rasmijn signaled agent Tromp to stand by at the door entrance.

"Please inspector Rasmijn, allow me to introduce us, my name is Prof. Arturo leyba from the Miskatonic University in Massachusetts, USA, this here is my assistant, Ms. Ashley Moore; the gentleman over there is Mr. Joao Manuel Figeiro, our ... how can I best describe him ... let's call him for now our special consultant, and of course the gentleman sitting in the couch is the owner of this house, Mr. Randolph Erasmus, whose case I'm sure you're familiar with. Please inspector, how can we be of any help."

It took a few seconds for inspector Rasmijn to regain his composure. "Eh ... yes, well ... we received several calls from neighbors reporting a group of strangers, no offence, odd individuals roaming around this house, which is already somewhat under investigation due to recent affairs. Can you explain the reason for your presence here? May I see your documents? Can you fill me in with respect to the reason of your visit to Aruba?"

Figeiro and Leyba briefly exchanged glances. Figeiro nodded. Ms. Moore looked at inspector Rasmijn while whispering to the professor, "We will need his help, Arturo. I'm afraid this time we're not able to pull this off alone. There are too many already involved."

"What is going on here..."

"Please inspector Rasmijn," Prof. Leyba interrupted him, "Allow me to fully explain the urgency and complexity of the situation at hand. We are running out of time, please sit right here on the sofa ... Ms. Moore, if you will please, can you show the inspector your special gift?"

Ms. Moore sat next to inspector Rasmijn and placed her right hand on his left arm. Rasmijn looked at her and his surrounding in increased impatience, and yet at the touch of her hand he felt a strange urge of curiosity, as if an inner voice told him to give these eccentrics the benefit of doubt. She slowly caressed his arm and then grabbed his left hand firmly. She closed her eyes.

"Rasmijn, Frederik Norman ... 47 years of age ... single ... one son ... named Mauricio ... currently 22 years and studying in Rotterdam, the Netherlands ... you graduated in 1985 at the Police Academy in Apeldoorn in Holland ... youngest inspector ever in the then Netherland Antilles ..."

"Pffft ... come on!" Rasmijn snapped as he tried to stand up. Ms. Moore however kept an iron grip.

"You accidently killed a junky in 1989. You then framed the situation to look like self defense. There is only one person on the island who knows this ... your then mentor inspector Gustavo Gonzalez who is now retired and in not so good mental health due to Alzheimer ..."

"Enough!"

Inspector Rasmijn jumped as if bitten by a snake. His hand was still firmly held by Ms. Moore as if glued with world's strongest epoxy.

"Enough, I said. Goddammit! Fuck ... let ... my ... hand ... go ..."

Special agent Oswaldo Tromp, who remained all the time in the doorway, quickly came forward with his right hand on his pistol at his side.

"Stop! Let the inspector go!"

"That's enough dear." Leyba said in a soft tone, while raising his hand gently in the direction of agent Tromp. Before both policemen could say or do anything, Prof. Leyba placed his arm on the inspector's shoulder and in the same soft tone he said: "Please inspector, forgive me for having upset you this way, there was no other way than to get straight to the point and demonstrate to you that what you are dealing here with is a very special situation."

Inspector Rasmijn, visibly still shaken by what he just experienced, nodded to agent Tromp indicating that he's okay.

Prof. Leyba directed inspector Rasmijn's attention to the large archaic book lying on the table. This instantly stopped Rasmijn in his tracks: he stared mesmerized at the book.

"Please inspector..." Prof. Leyba whispered. "Please bear with me and allow me to explain our presence here and how we may save, Mr. Erasmus, your island, and humankind itself from great danger."

Rasmijn took a deep breath and sat quietly in front of the mysterious book. "You have my attention, doctor," he whispered, eyes still fixated on the book. "As weird as this may sound, I'm willing to hear you out, as I have seen this book before ... in a strange and inexplicable series of bizarre dreams I have been experiencing lately."

A deep disturbing rumble could be heard far away in the distance. Like echoes of a rolling thunder miles away. Timmy moved restless and visibly shaken by the ominous sound. Prof. Leyba looked at his watch. Time was rapidly running short.

"Inspector Rasmijn," he said with a worried and troubled look on his face. "Please do not take the following words lightly, or as the ramblings of a man living on the edge of insanity. Many eons ago our universe, and hence this planet, was ruled by *the ancient ones*, mythical god like cosmological beings whose existence still echo through modern times by means of myths and sagas which can be found in all cultures around the globe. The Greeks spoke of Titans who ruled the earth and existed before the Gods. Similar concepts of ancient deities can be found in Hindu, Babylonian, Mayan, Aztec, Norse and many other mythologies. The issue at hand here, Mr. Rasmijn, is that mankind *thinks* it knows how the universe works. However, mankind lives on a placid island of ignorance amid black seas of infinity, where it wasn't meant we should voyage far. I wish I could explain a lot more, however, time is of the essence if tonight we are to prevent the horrors bestowed on mankind if these archaic beings fulfill their mission."

Prof. Leyba opens the Necronomicon and quickly navigates to a page earmarked in the center.

"Allow me to read to you about what I think we are dealing with tonight, Inspector Rasmijn. If Mr. Figeiro here, who carefully analyzed Mr. Erasmus's dreams, is not mistaken, we are dealing with no less than *Yog-Sothoth*, one of the very most powerful *Ancient Ones*. I quote:

'Nor is it to be thought that man is either the oldest or the last of earth's masters, or that the common bulk of life and substances walks alone. The Old Ones were, the Old Ones are, and the Old Ones shall be. Not in the spaces we know, but between them, They walk serene and primal, un-dimensioned and to us unseen. Yog-Sothoth knows the gate. Yog-Sothoth is the gate. Yog-Sothoth is the key and guardian of the gate. Past, present, future, all are one in Yog-Sothoth. He knows where the Old Ones broke through of old, and where They shall break through again. He knows where They have trod earth's fields, and where They still tread them, and why no one can behold Them as They tread. By Their smell can men sometimes know them near, but of Their semblance can no man know, saving only in the features of those They have begotten on mankind; and of those are there many sorts, differing in likeness from man's truest eidolon to that shape without sight or substance which is Them. They walk unseen and foul in lonely places where the Words have been spoken and the Rites howled through at their Seasons. The wind gibbers with Their voices, and the earth mutters with Their consciousness. They bend the forest and crush the city, yet may not forest or city behold the hand that smites. Kadath in the cold waste hath known Them, and what man knows Kadath? The ice desert of the South and the sunken isles of Ocean hold stones where Their seal is engraven, but who hath seen the deep frozen city or the sealed tower long garlanded with seaweed and barnacles? Great Cthulhu is Their cousin, yet can he spy Them only dimly. Iä! Shub-Niggurath! As a foulness shall ye know Them. Their hand is at your throats, yet ye see Them not; and Their habitation is even one with your guarded threshold. Yog-Sothoth is the key to the gate, whereby the spheres meet. Man rules now where They ruled once; They shall soon rule where man rules now. After summer is winter, and after winter summer. They wait patient and potent, for here shall They reign again.'

The deep rumble in the distance could be heard again. This time louder, as if steadfastly approaching.

"Professor ..." Timmy whispered.

"I know, Timmy, I know ... Inspector Rasmijn," the professor continued, "we are in great danger. You must take my word for it. These archaic deities, these infernal creatures beyond any imagination, move in *inter-dimensional spacetime*. They are extra-terrestrial beings with enormous powers. This may come as a shock to you inspector, but the universe doesn't give a shit about you, me, or us. There are forces out there beyond our comprehension that have total disregard for our existence. We are nothing, mere microbes to these beings. They want what once belonged to them, and they will keep trying to breach into our dimension at all cost, and tonight, if we don't at least attempt to stop them with all our strength, they will succeed in bringing unspeakable horror to us all."

Inspector Rasmijn leaned back into his chair and grasped his head firmly between his two hands. "This is beyond anyone's capacity to take ..." he whispered.

Figeiro stood up and went to him. Rasmijn's stomach revolted at the sight and smell of Figeiro's face so close to his own. A strange repulsive stench reached his nose when Figeiro spoke to him up close.

"Rasmijn, do you know what happens to you when you fall asleep? Do you know who is trying to access your mind and attempts to influence your thoughts, your very essence as a human being? Are those inexplicable thoughts and images you call dreams really yours?"

Rasmijn stared at Figeiro's grotesque face in bewilderment.

"Tell me Rasmijn ... do you really know what enters and crawls inside your head every time you so innocently surrender yourself to what you think will be a good night sleep? If you only knew what I have seen exists out there in the infinite vastness of the cosmos. What is happening right now is that the *Ancient One* known as *Yog-Sothoth, the keeper of the gate,* has found a way to create a tiny rift in the spacetime continuum via Mr. Erasmus's unconscious brain when asleep. *Yog-Sothoth* has succeeded in making Mr. Erasmus's brain resonate unconsciously with *Yog-Sothoth* conscious essence in another dimension, and tonight my dear inspector, *It* intends to deepen that rift so that *They* can get through and obtain a foothold in our dimension. It's a process that has been attempted over and over again through history, and once in a while they reach a fertile brain. And this book," Figeiro slaps his palm hard on the cover of the *Necronomicon*, "is all that stands tonight between our world and them!"

It took some time before things slowly began to sink in with the inspector. Timmy began to become more restless with each passing minute and every time the rumble in the distance became louder and sounded more ominous. At a certain moment, those with ears sharp enough instantly noticed the difference: there was a strange undertone, a weird and menacing roar. Figeiro instantly turned his head into the direction it came from; Timmy, visibly in panic, rushed to him and grasped his hand firmly.

Special agent Tromp entered the room, went to the inspector and whispered something in his ear. They both left outside, where special agent Tromp pointed out something in the distant Southern horizon to inspector Rasmijn, who, after staring a few moments in total disbelief, rushed back inside.

"Prof. Leyba, you better come outside and look at this. Whatever it is, it looks like *Catatumbo*[31] itself is moving towards us."

All of them went outside except for Figeiro and Timmy who hastily went to the *Necronomicon*, opened it and began searching for the rite passages.

"It's happening ..." Prof. Leyba said. Looking towards the Southern horizon, he could clearly see the massive carmine clouds distinguish themselves against the early evening sky.

"*It* will be here soon," he continued. "We must be prepared. I hope you can help us out, Inspector Rasmijn. Your assistance will be invaluable tonight."

"I have no clue whatsoever how this all is going to play out professor, but my gut feeling tells me I better start choosing sides. Tell me what you need, *prófe*."

With eyes still fixed to the Southern horizon, Prof. Leyba said: "You will need to address the people of this island quickly.

---

[31] The Catatumbo region at Lake Maracaibo, Venezuela, is well known for a weird atmospheric phenomena where regions of thunder clouds form at a height of over 1 km over the mouth of the Catatumbo river. These massive storm cells occur around 140 to 160 nights per year, with lightning strikes of over 280 times per hour for more than 10 hours straight. It is generally referred to as *The Catatumbo Lightning*. Prussian naturalist and explorer Alexander von Humboldt described the lightning in 1826. Italian geographer Agustin Codazzi described it in 1841 as "like a continuous lightning, and its position such that, located almost on the meridian of the mouth of the lake, it directs the navigators as a lighthouse."
The phenomenon is depicted on the flag and coat of arms of the state of Zulia which also contains Lake Maracaibo, and is mentioned in the state's anthem. The phenomenon has been known for centuries as the "Lighthouse of Maracaibo", since it is visible for miles around Lake Maracaibo.

Send a communiqué with the utmost urgency telling everyone to remain inside their houses. Use the unexpected atmospheric condition as a pretext. Stress the urgency of the matter and emphasize that they must brace themselves inside closed quarters, and above all, that they must not go outside or fall asleep. The last thing we'll need are accessible minds."

"Professor! Professor! Come quick!" Leyba heard Timmy screaming inside the house. They all ran back inside. Randolph Erasmus was lying on the floor. His eyes were rolled up in the back of his head, and his mouth was one huge blob of foam of a strange and hideous color.

※ ※ ※ ※

"Y'AI'NG'NGAH,
YOG-SOTHOTH
H'EE-L'GEB
F'AI THRODOG
UAAAH"

Figeiro was reading this chant out loud from page 587 of the *Necronomicon*. By now, after 2 hours of incessant chanting, all of the others knew the required reply by heart. In chorus they replied like exhausted zombies:

"OGTHROD AI'F
GEB'L-EE'H
YOG-SOTHOTH
'NGAH'NG AI'Y
ZHRO"

They were all standing in a circle around Randolph Erasmus who was lying on his back strapped on top of the table in the dining room. Randolph's eyes were wide open, but only the white of his eyes were visible. His mouth was gurning constantly in the most horrendous ways while his face was contorting into one horrifying grimace after the other. At some point, special agent Tromp had to cover his mouth not to throw up at the rank odor emanating from the foam bubbling constantly with a gurgling sound from Randolph's gaping mouth. At a certain moment Prof. Leyba yelled at him between the chant's replies to stay focused, but it was too late. The sight and smell, and especially the abominable taste it created in his mouth, were too much for agent Tromp. He ran outside only to remain paralyzed by the spectacle he witnessed high in the sky.

The clouds above Oranjestad seemed to be filled with red embers and were circling in a frenzy around a pitch black hole in the center. A thousand lightning bolts were radiating in all directions, illuminating the deep red-orange glow of the thick clouds with a hallucinating shade of metallic blue. A thick sulphur like smell was penetrating every orifice for miles around. Heavy thunder was pounding the ground every minute or so, making the whole city shake to its core. The hurricane-like wind was howling like a thousand wolves in heat. Special agent Tromp fell to his knees and grabbed his head between his two hands in a futile attempt to close his ears. From deep inside his throat, he let out a primordial scream which instantly diffused in the chaotic cacophony all around him.

Agent Tromp felt a hand grab him firmly by the neck. It was Ms. Moore.

"You must come back inside!" she yelled at him with all her strength. "If you stay here you will die!"

Her eyes were blood shot red. A strange bluish hue was glowing deep inside the center of her eyes. Her teeth were protruding slowly from an evil grin which gradually expanded over her face. Black saliva started to ooze from her gums dripping on her chin.

"No!" special agent Tromp screamed his lungs out. "Get away from me!"

"You must get inside! We cannot remain here!"

Special agent Tromp could barely hear her above the pandemonium surrounding both. Her face was close by his and he could smell the breathtaking stench originating from the tar like saliva bubbling out of her mouth. With each thundering lightning strike, her teeth seemed to grow larger, shimmering with an ever hypnotizing bluish hue.

In a desperate move, special agent Tromp wrestled himself loose from her grip, took a big step backward, grabbed his gun and pointed it towards her.

"Get back! Get back or I'll shoot!"

"You don't understand ... I'm begging you, come with me inside, you don't stand a chance here ... you must ..."

Special agent Tromp fired, hitting her point blank in the chest; the sound and flash of the 44 magnum evaporating into the chaotic madness all around him. The strong wind got hold of Ms. Moore's lifeless body and rolled her as she sank like a rag doll to the ground.

Inside the house, Timmy jerked upwards, eyes wide open screaming "No, no, no, noooooo ..."

"Leyba!" Figeiro screamed. Prof. Leyba just nodded. A deep sad look came into his eyes. He has felt it too. Ms. Moore was gone.

Outside, special agent Tromp was staring in total disbelief at Ms. Moore's body. He dropped his gun and fell to his knees.

'*What happened? How is this possible?*' went through his mind as he caressed her beautiful face. Where were the horrendous teeth? What happened to the tar like saliva? All that remained in the whirling air was a faint smell of her perfume. In absolute dismay he kept staring at her angelic appearance lying on the ground, her skirt fluttering wildly in the howling wind.

"Tromp!"

The deep growling voice startled him. He looked up and saw a dark figure standing in the door opening. Its obscure face seemed covered with octopus-like tentacles and huge wings were protruding from behind.

"Tromp!" it growled again. "You must get back inside! Leave her, there is nothing more you can do. We need you inside!"

Special agent Tromp picked up his gun and wildly fired a shot in the direction of the winged creature. The bullet missed the head of Prof. Leyba standing in the door's opening by a mere inch and hit the wooden frame. Another shot followed. Leyba quickly jumped inside. The bullet missed and exploded in the wall behind him.

"Rasmijn!" he screamed.

Inspector Rasmijn looked outside and saw special agent Tromp walking slowly towards the house, pistol firmly held by both hands in firing position.

"You must take him out, Rasmijn," Leyba said lying on the floor.

"I can't do that ... he ... he is ..."

"For God's sake man, he has lost it out there. He is totally hallucinating. He has fallen under *Its* control."

Rasmijn stepped outside, arms raised high above his head.

"Tromp, it's me," he yelled in vain into the howling wind.

Special agent Tromp stopped in his tracks. With eyes squinting, he saw this huge amorphous creature standing in front of him, with hundreds of tentacles raised to the thundering sky and with countless glasslike eyes held at the end of each wriggling tentacle.

"Tromp it's me," he heard the creature growl again, and with eyes wide in maniacal panic he fired several shots which miraculously missed inspector Rasmijn by a hair's width.

"Rasmijn," Leyba shouted against the howling wind, "Do something for Christ's sake. He's not himself anymore, can't you see that? Put him down before he reaches us. He already killed Moore; he will do us all. Get a hold of yourself, do something!"

Rasmijn looked up to the sky above and instantly froze, like a rabbit in a car's head lights. That light, the beauty of it ... the immense power radiating from those ember colored clouds spinning in an insane whirlpool ... thousands of lightning strikes radiating to all edges of the horizon ... that hypnotizing undertone accompanying each thunder clap pounding the earth ... that unnatural high pitched howling of the wind ... he raised his arms higher, screaming words in an unknown tongue...

A sharp pain in his left leg made him buckle and come back to earth. Special agent Tromp was approaching fast and was firing again. Rasmijn went for his gun and tried to aim at the out of control agent walking towards him, but the sharp pain in his left leg made it impossible to steady his hand. He felt Prof. Leyba's arm grab him under his left armpit and with the other hand steady his right hand holding the gun in order to obtain a better aim.

"*Dios pordonami*," Rasmijn whispered and emptied the gun's clip. Special agent Tromp managed to make one last step and then fall eyes wide open to his knees, asking "why?"

"Whatever you do, don't look to the sky," Prof. Leyba shouted in his ears. "We have to get back inside. Now. There is nothing you can do any..."

"Leybaaaaaa!" Figeiro's scream from inside the house was barely audible.

"We have to go inside. Now!" Prof. Leyba insisted adamantly.

Inspector Rasmijn just nodded, looking like a man about to lose the last ounce of sanity left in his mind.

❊   ❊   ❊   ❊

"Y'AI'NG'NGAH,
YOG-SOTHOTH
H'EE-L'GEB
F'AI THRODOG
UAAAH"

"OGTHROD AI'F
GEB'L-EE'H
YOG-SOTHOTH
'NGAH'NG AI'Y
ZHRO"

Figeiro and Timmy were chanting the secret rites of the *Necronomicon* in an ever increasing frantic pace, while with a huge effort Prof. Leyba was attempting to stem the bleeding at Rasmijn's left leg. Leyba worked in a hurry, sweating profusely. He knew he had to get back as soon as possible to join the chant, and if possible, bring in Rasmijn as well to increase their ranks. The loss of Ms. Moore has weakened them considerably. How regrettable this fact may be, Leyba still hoped all was not lost.

He stood up and helped Rasmijn in a chair. "No matter how weak you may feel," he told Rasmijn, "do participate with everything left in you. We are weak without Moore, but we are not defeated yet."

Leyba grabbed Timmy's right hand and Rasmijn's left hand with his other hand. Figeiro joined by taking Rasmijn's right hand with his left hand. The chanting continued incessantly ...

"Y'AI'NG'NGAH,
YOG-SOTHOTH
H'EE-L'GEB
F'AI THRODOG
UAAAH"

"OGTHROD AI'F
GEB'L-EE'H
YOG-SOTHOTH
'NGAH'NG AI'Y
ZHRO"

Over and over, again and again, hour after hour, the four went at it. Their voices strength infused by massive amount of adrenaline. Each time Rasmijn was fading into unconsciousness Leyba would scream at him or even press into his left leg's wound. The excruciating pain would jolt him back into joining them. Hours crept by slowly ... their voices held, no matter how heavy their eyelids felt ... at the end the howling outside slowly subdued, the thunder became less and less loud and more away in the distance; the constant bluish flickering of the lightning outside gradually became a thing of the past.

❖ ❖ ❖ ❖

It was around 8 o'clock in the morning that Inspector Rasmijn opened his eyes. A nurse was tending his wound. The excruciating pain was now a distant throb. An empty ampoule on the table next to the sofa explained it all: the morphine it contained was already doing its job through his veins.

Next to him, sat Chief Inspector Jorge Werleman. He had a troubled look on his face. "How are you feeling," he said.

Rasmijn nodded a bit confused. In the corner at the far side of the room he saw two detectives taking notes while talking to Prof. Leyba, Mr. Figeiro, and Randolph Erasmus. Probably taking their statement, he thought. Who was going to believe them? How are they ever to explain the incredible events of last night? He sighed and closed his eyes. *This was going to be a long day.* Chief Inspector Werleman confirmed his fears.

"You have a lot to explain amigo," Chief Inspector Werleman said, "and to be honest, I'm a bit worried how your side of the story will go down."

Rasmijn nodded again.

Chief Inspector Werleman leaned forward. "We have a major situation on our hands here," he whispered. "The Prime Minister is breathing down my neck. The Governor, and thus The Hague, are on the Prime Minister's back and ready to intervene if he doesn't come up with any satisfactory explanations. As you already know, shit rolls downhill and it's coming down at avalanche speed. Just to give you any idea what we're up against, last night looked like right out of the movie *The Purge*. For incomprehensible reasons, almost everyone who was outside in the open during the storm tried to kill each other. Many policemen who were on patrol, instead of controlling the situation, went completely bananas and started shooting at everything that moved, even their own partners."

Rasmijn closed his eyes and cringed.

"To make things worse," Chief Inspector Werleman continued in an anxious tone, "we lost many tourists in the low rise hotel area. You know what a delicate matter dead tourists are on the island. This is gonna hurt big time."

"How come only in the low rise area?"

"That's the strangest thing of all," Chief Inspector Werleman answered. "The further the distance from this area, the less violent and chaotic the situation became. For instance, in San Nicolas there were only a few incidences. It's like the epicenter was right here above this house or at least this area. That's why we came here. We literary had to just follow the ravage and dead bodies. Besides, from where I was located I could clearly see that *thing* hovering for hours above this area, churning out weird lightning and thunder as I've never seen before."

Rasmijn nodded again, silently. After a brief pause, he asked, "Where were you stationed?"

"At the Santa Cruz headquarters. I was overseeing the national alert you requested, when all of a sudden things rapidly started to turn crazy. Calls were coming in from all over the island that people were killing each other on the streets. Officers on patrol were calling in that they were being shot at by their own partner. It was ... it was ..."

Inspector Rasmijn let out a deep sigh. The whole thing was just too much for words. Both men looked at each other. "What's next chief. Tell me what to do. Tell me what you need. We are in deep shit. Nobody is going to believe what happened here. What we saw. What we went through. Agent Tromp shot and killed a member of the professor's group. The press is gonna have a ball; a policeman killing a tourist. After that, Tromp kept shooting at me like a maniac ... as if he was scared beyond his wits by me ... by... by something ... I had to shoot him, chief, there was no other way. It was either him or me ... I tried to talk to him ... I ..."

Werleman put a hand on Rasmijn's shoulder. "I know ... I mean, I believe you," he said. "I already spoke with Prof. Leyba. His account of whatever happened here doesn't make any sense at all, but at least he claims he witnessed most of what happened outside during the shootout. He was adamant you acted in self-defense. I also talked to Mr. Erasmus, but his memory was a complete blank. Leyba explained to me why."

Chief Inspector Werleman leaned closer towards Rasmijn's ear. "Here's what I think we ought to do," he whispered. "First of all we'll take you to the hosp—"

"I'm okay," Rasmijn interrupted.

"No you're not. Besides, most of those idiots from the press outside, who have been swarming like ants around the house since dawn, will follow the ambulance to the hospital. You are not to talk to the press under any circumstances. Is that clear?"

Rasmijn nodded.

"Good. I already instructed PR to take care of them, whatever it takes, so your trip to the ER will help. Secondly, I'll remain here with the professor, that creepy looking Figeiro, and that strange boy. When things calm down, I'll take them to headquarters in Santa Cruz for thorough questioning. No use dragging Erasmus into this for the time being. The man already went through hell as I understand, and besides, he doesn't seem to remember shit. You will join us there this afternoon. Together, I hope the five of us can come up with a story, at least some credible explanation, of all this madness."

By noon, most of the early morning chaos began to clear up. The coroner's office took care of both special agent Tromp as well as Ms. Moore's body in order to perform the necessary autopsies. Most detectives were done taking statements from the few neighbors who managed to witness anything during last night's chaotic events, and they had already left. Things gradually returned to normal, if that could ever be possible after such an Armageddon like night.

By early afternoon Fahrenheitstraat was open for traffic again. The public works department managed to clean up pretty much all the debris and rubbish left behind by the unnatural storm. Randolph Erasmus was standing in the front doorway. Prof. Arturo Leyba, Timmy, and the enigmatic Mr. Figeiro were just a few feet further outside the house on the front lawn. On the street in front of the house, the Toyota Prado police patrol SUV was parked next to the curb; its engine running; Chief Inspector Werleman waiting impatiently for the group to say goodbye to Erasmus.

Mr. Figeiro took a long look at Randolph Erasmus. He stepped forward and shook Randolph's hand saying, "It took great courage to do what you did last night, Mr. Erasmus. Some of the sights and sounds you must have experienced while battling those cosmic horrors would have driven anyone else to complete insanity. You stood for hours at the mouth of madness and stared into its most hideous manifestations. And yet here you are, visibly exhausted but showing an iron will to head forward and get on with your life. You have fought hard and brave for that privilege, I commend you, Mr. Erasmus."

Randolph took a bow with his head and with trembling voice he said, "Thank you Mr. Figeiro. I ... I know now what you must have witnessed for many years. I am in great debt with you sir. Part of my soul is forever bonded with yours. Thank you for saving me."

Figeiro nodded with sad understanding eyes. "Not only you, Randolph, but humankind in its totality," he whispered and slowly let go of Randolph's hand.

Prof. Leyba stepped forward and placed his hands on Randolph's shoulders while looking him straight in the eye. "I wish you well, my friend. It will take some time before the nightmares extinguish. Be patient. Be strong. Never give up."

Randolph nodded. Tears started to well in his eyes. "I'm sorry for your loss," he whispered.

Prof. Leyba remained silent for a brief moment. "We have lost an irreplaceable member of our team. She will be greatly missed. It wasn't your fault, Randolph, you're not to blame yourself. You haven't opted for all this, *They* have chosen you to attempt to create a rift through which they can enter. You must remain always on your guard, amigo. Always. *They* don't tend to let go easily, but you're stronger now and better prepared than before."

Randolph nodded affirmatively. "Goodbye, professor."

"Not goodbye my friend. *Auf wiedersehen* ... until we meet again."

Timmy hugged Randolph, his head barely reaching Randolph's lower chest. "Goodbye Mr. Erasmus."

"Goodbye, my little amigo."

Timmy moved his head slightly sideways to his right. He peered for a brief moment into the house to the wall at the far side of the room behind Randolph's back. He then pressed his face back unto Randolph's lower chest and muttered, "Stay safe Mr. Erasmus ..."

Chief Inspector Werleman honked twice announcing that their time was running short. After a last shake of hands, they all went to the police SUV and entered it, Timmy last. Before doing so, he turned around and waved for the last time to Randolph, who was still standing in the door way, waving back.

The police SUV started moving. Timmy pressed his face against the rear window, trying to catch a last glimpse of Randolph, still in the doorway, still waving. Unnoticeable to all in the police SUV, the wall at the far side of the room behind Randolph's back appeared to start moving. The bright afternoon sun was in stark contrast with the darkness inside the house, where glistening eyes appeared to be opening one by one against the wall, which gradually seemed to morph into a vertical malleable glob with an uncanny deep hue of dark blue.

A thin hideous grin slowly appeared on Randolph's face. His teeth seemed more pointed than before. At the wall at his back to the far side of the room, the wall enveloped in darkness was by now almost completely covered with eyes, all of them blinking asynchronously, like a surreal decoration created by Salvador Dali. A deep thundering voice at the wall resonated with a strange reverb.

"Do you think we managed to get away this time?"

"Yes ...," Randolph nodded, the grin on his face increasing in size and malice. "I think this time we've finally pulled it off ..."

At the end of the street the police SUV suddenly stopped, braking hard with a loud shriek. Chief Inspector Werleman put on the signal light indicating he was to turn right, and waited impatiently at the approaching car he noticed just in time. Timmy turned around and stared in a pensive way in front of him. When the police SUV pulled up and turned to the right, Timmy turned and gave a long look at Mr. Figeiro sitting next to him. Those hideous scars, the hundreds of tiny spider web like wrinkles; a thousand battles and million moments of agony and pain behind those dark piercing eyes. Timmy nodded slowly, as if finally realizing he was looking at a future version of himself; acknowledging the long and arduous journey that lay ahead. He thought about Ms. Moore. Such a brave, brilliant angel, in this eons lasting battle. Alas, no chess game has ever been won without pieces being moved forward and occasionally getting knocked down, he thought. A thousand battles, a million moments of agony and pain, he pondered while almost inaudibly whispering: "*Au revoir, monsieur Erasmus* ... until we meet again."

The End.